'How long do we have to stay here?'

He watched her elegant throat work around a swallow. 'Why?'

'Because t̶̶̶̶̶̶̶̶̶̶ else I'd much rather be doing r̶

'Oh?' she a saucy little smi̶

Tommy lea̶ ll her, watching as her lips par̶ ̶w flushed and her breath caught.

'And where, exactly, do you propose we do all, um, that?'

'Wait a couple of minutes, then follow me out.'

He placed his champagne glass on the table, straightened his suit jacket, then strode from the room without a second glance.

It took every ounce of self-restraint Jena possessed not to follow Tommy the instant he turned to leave. Four days had passed since she'd found him on her doorstep like a tasty morsel just waiting to be devoured. But rather than getting her fill of him, every moment that passed increased the risk of that same desire overwhelming her entirely. A new emotion for her. And a dangerously exciting one.

Dear Reader,

Jena McCade is a woman who knows what she wants and takes it. Wouldn't we all like to say that about ourselves? Have you ever wondered why so many of us can't? Perhaps it's because we're afraid of finding ourselves smack-dab in the middle of a situation that may be too hot to handle. That's what happens to our heroine. Because Tommy Brodie should come with a warning label – *Caution: Live Wire.*

In *Fire and Ice*, provocative criminal defence attorney Jena McCade has faced her share of opponents in the courtroom, but sexy Tommy 'Wild Man' Brodie is her toughest opponent yet in the personal arena. When a scorching one-night stand leaves Tommy thinking he can take up permanent residence in her life, Jena uses every weapon in her arsenal to scare him off. Only Tommy's made of stronger stuff than that. And when he utilises a few of his own sexual weapons…well, Jena never stands a chance.

We hope you enjoy Jena and Tommy's sizzling story. We'd love to hear what you think. Write to us at PO Box 12271, Toledo, OH 43612, USA, or visit us at www.toricarrington.com. And don't miss Marie's story, *Going Too Fa*r, available in March 2004.

Here's wishing you happy (and hot!) reading!

Lori and Tony Karayianni

aka Tori Carrington

FIRE AND ICE

by

Tori Carrington

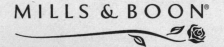
MILLS & BOON®

This one's for List Mistress Extraordinaire Barb Hicks and the
whole crew at ToriCarringtonFriends@yahoogroups.com.

Thank you, thank you and thank you again for your unwavering
support, friendship and for the great water balloon fights!

Our heartfelt gratitude, as well, to our editor Brenda Chin.
She knows why.

*First published in Great Britain 2004
by Harlequin Mills & Boon Limited,
Eton House, 18-24 Paradise Road, Richmond, Surrey TW9 1SR*

© Lori and Tony Karayianni 2002

ISBN 0 263 84044 1

14-0204

*Printed and bound in Spain
by Litografia Rosés S.A., Barcelona*

1

THE FRICTION OF SKIN against skin sliding one way then the other. Chest tight, nipples bunched into tight points, sending shivers cascading over her body. Stomach trembling, limbs languid yet restless. The sense of moving toward something terrifying and freeing all at once gathered deep in her belly, making her want to pull back and rush toward that place at the same time. Her wet tongue darted out, flicking hungrily over her bottom lip as her breathing grew shallow, air more difficult to come by.

Air whooshed, but not from Jena McCade's tingling lips. Rather she blinked to find that she wasn't in the king-size hotel bed she had spent the night in three months ago with hockey player Tommy ''Wild Man'' Brodie. Rather she was in her office at Lomax, Ferris, McCade and Bertelli, Attorneys-at-Law on a gray Monday morning in late November. And Mona Lyndell, the secretary they all shared, had just dropped an overstuffed manila folder on top of Jena's desk.

Jena's cheeks burned as she took a deep, calming breath. She managed a smile at the fifty-something secretary. "Talk about your daydreams," she whispered.

A frown marred Mona's clean brow as she smoothed back her salt-and-pepper hair that was ceaselessly pulled into a bun. The style reminded Jena of something an old schoolmarm would wear. Only she couldn't remember any of her teachers looking like Mona. Instead it looked like something she might have seen in an old *Little House on the Prairie* episode.

"I was talking about depositions," the secretary said.

Mona had been talking? Boy, she was in worse shape than she'd thought. Not only hadn't she heard Mona come in but apparently she'd missed an entire conversation.

"Depositions," Jena said aloud, trying to jerk her mind away from the heat of her thighs generated by her rubbing them together during her daydream. "Yes." She pulled the file in front of her. "Good. Good. The lead witness deposition in the Glendale case."

"Just came in by messenger ten minutes ago."

"Very good."

Mona lingered a moment longer.

"What?" Jena said, sounding irritatingly snippy even to herself, which was definitely not normal. When she was snippy she usually intended to be.

Mona's brows lifted above her large-framed wire glasses. "Did I say anything?"

"No, but I know that look."

"I was just going to ask if everything was okay. Lately, you seem to be, well...I guess distracted is the word I'm looking for."

Oh, she was distracted all right. But she wasn't about to share the reason for that unfortunate state with Mona. Not that she thought the secretary couldn't keep a secret. Rather she was having a hard time coming to terms with her borderline adolescent musings. She *did*, not fantasized about doing it.

Jena eyed the now even larger pile of papers regarding the Patsy Glendale murder case taking up the better half of her desk. "Have you given any thought to what I said yesterday?"

Mona's spine snapped slightly straighter—if that were possible. "You mean about my hair color?"

Jena knew her best friend and partner would absolutely kill her for saying something like this to the older woman. Dulcy Ferris would tell her she was being callous and controlling. The thing of it was Jena thought she was being helpful.

So, okay, the suggestion that Mona might want to reconsider her decision to age naturally and instead look into a good colorist—had even given the secretary the name of her own hairdresser—had come on the heels of an incident just like the one they were experiencing now. Jena had been daydreaming about

Tommy, Mona had come in on some urgent business matter or another, and Jena had made the comment on her hair.

And now she was following up on it.

"It was just a thought, Mona." She sighed, briefly propping her head on her hand, then shoving her fingers through the fine, jet-black strands of her shoulder-length hair. "I can only imagine what you think of the comment."

"Is that an apology?"

Jena smiled. "No. It's a statement of fact."

"I see."

Jena noted the glimmer of amusement in the other woman's eyes, although there was no way that Mona could know that much of Jena's state was due to one singular night of passion with a man she hadn't seen since...well, that night.

Her. Jena. A woman unafraid of her own sexuality who changed men as often as she changed her bed sheets, preoccupied with a man who had so clearly been a one-night stand. In fact, he not only wasn't in her life...he wasn't even in the same city.

Which hockey team had he played on? Oh, yes. The L.A. Aces. Fitting, since Tommy was the highest scoring card in her black book. Not only did he live up to all the things she'd said about hockey players having, um, big sticks and being smooth, he'd surpassed them. And then some.

Mona cleared her throat. "I'll be at my desk if you need anything."

Jena waved her hand. "Thanks, Mona."

The instant the secretary exited the office, Jena wanted to groan aloud.

She made an attempt at continuing the notes she was making on a secondary case but the words refused to make sense. A latent case of dyslexia? Hardly.

Okay, so the sex with Tommy had been good. Great. Mind-blowingly fantastic. But it wasn't like her to revisit one-night stands, even in her daydreams. And, for cripes' sake, the night had been in September and now it was late November. She glanced out her office-wide window. She supposed part of the reason for her overheated, sappy condition was that things had been quiet on the dating front as of late.

Well, actually, things had been nonexistent ever since...

Ever since three months ago.

She nearly choked at the revelation. No, that wasn't possible. She'd dated since then, hadn't she? She swiveled her chair to the bureau behind her desk and took her purse out of a drawer, rifling through it for her Day-Timer. Surely she'd gone out since then? Had some sort of midnight encounter?

Yes, yes. There was that John Pollero she'd met at a gallery opening.

She flipped through the pages of her personal calendar, but aside from the notations of her monthly menstrual cycle, white paper stared back at her.

But she was sure…

There was the notation. She'd gone out to dinner with John a week before Dulcy's bachelorette party and Jena's night with Tommy.

She pulled a face, refusing to admit it.

So she'd grown lax in keeping her Day-Timer up to date. She slapped it back into her bag then the bureau. That was all. She'd never gone three months without some sort of interaction with the opposite sex. She adored men and loved sex. Especially great sex with adorable men. She'd merely forgotten to note the dates, that's all. After all, as Dulcy and Marie constantly told her, others found it impossible to keep up with her. It was understandable that she was having trouble keeping up with herself.

''Knock, knock,'' Dulcy Ferris said from her open doorway.

Jena blinked at her incredibly blond, incredibly beautiful friend, then frowned. Something she seemed to be doing a lot of lately whenever she ran into one of her two best friends.

''Who's there?'' she said wryly.

Dulcy laughed quietly then stepped into the room. ''Well, obviously no one worth mentioning given the expression on your face.''

''Never mind me. It's this Glendale murder case, that's all.''

"Are you sure?"

"How do you mean?"

Dulcy sat down in one of the two high-back leather chairs in front of Jena's desk. Chairs she'd bought when she was on the track to partnership at Scott, Dickey and Jolson, one of Albuquerque's premier law offices. The long hours, the cutthroat competition, the high-profile cases, the drive to succeed seemed to have all happened long ago, although barely nine months had passed since she and Dulcy and Marie had resigned from their respective jobs as attorneys and signed on with Bartholomew Lomax, fulfilling a lifelong dream of running their own firm. With Lomax's help and weight in the legal community, they did so without having to build from the ground up. Barry came with a long list of established and well-paying clients and a reputation that would have taken the three women years to shape.

Dulcy and Barry went way back, but Jena was still a bit fuzzy on the full extent of their relationship. No, there was nothing sexual between the sixty-something Lomax and her thirty-year-old friend, but the two shared a close connection Jena couldn't figure out.

"And here I thought I was the one having trouble concentrating," Dulcy said, tugging Jena from her reverie.

"Hmm?" She watched as Dulcy smoothed her hand over her flat stomach, reminding her that her friend was nearly three months pregnant and had good reason to be distracted, what with that American Indian stud of a husband of hers waiting for her at home. Of course, a dusty old horse ranch a good three hours outside of town wasn't Jena's idea of a good time, but she had the feeling Dulcy's husband Quinn Landis could make anyplace seem like a sexual playground built for two.

"It's been awhile since we've had a chance to talk," Dulcy said, "what with my commuting to the ranch every Wednesday night and returning Sunday." She caught herself rubbing her stomach and smiled. She put her hand on the armrest. "So who's the man of the hour?"

Jena was still staring at her friend's stomach.

"Hmm?"

"You know, who's the hottie you're dating now?"

Now that was the question of the hour, wasn't it?

"Okay. Let me try to narrow the parameters of my question a bit. Last night, who did you go to the Mc-Clellan reception with?"

Jena shrugged, attempting nonchalance although she was a little irked by the reminder. "No one."

"No one as in no one worth mentioning?"

"No one as in…well, no one."

"You didn't meet anyone there?"

"Nope."

"You didn't meet anyone worth pursuing?"

"Not even worth a second glance."

Dulcy looked skeptical. "Okay, what's going on?

I haven't heard you brag about any sexual conquests for at least a couple of weeks.'' She made a face. ''Actually, I think it's longer than that. Odd.''

Definitely odd, Jena admitted inwardly. In fact, she found it terrifyingly strange that she couldn't remember one single male face from the McClellan reception. She, the woman who usually surveyed a room the instant she entered it, sizing up every male in the place then putting them into selection order. Choice number one. Choice number two.

Jena felt Dulcy's very penetrating gaze on her. ''What?'' she said in much the same way as she had to Mona.

Dulcy shook her head, wearing the same amused expression Mona had. ''Oh, nothing. It's just that, well, your behavior lately has been a little outside the norm, that's all.''

Jena vaguely wished that Dulcy had reacted the same way Mona had, namely with a smile as she left her office.

''Maybe I just need to get laid.''

Dulcy's bark of laughter made Jena smile. ''God, that is such a man thing to say.''

''Not something I could see Quinn saying.''

Dulcy twisted her lips and tucked her pretty blond hair behind her ear. ''No. But we weren't talking about my man. We were discussing yours. You know, the type you tend to go out with.''

''The type just looking to get laid.''

"Uh-huh."

Jena squinted at her friend. "What's going on? It's not like you to fish for intimate details. You're usually telling me when to stop—which, I might add, is the instant I get started."

Dulcy shrugged her shoulders and leaned back in the chair. "Yes, well, I was just noticing that you hadn't even tried to share anything recently."

"And you missed it?"

"No, I was just wondering what brought about the change."

Jena found her gaze drawn to the window and the nearby Sandia Mountains. "I wish I knew."

"Well, at least Caramel is keeping you company."

Jena gave an exasperated sigh. "No, Caramel is making my life a living hell," she said of the four-month-old puppy Dulcy had given to her a month ago. A blond boxer, it had to be one of the ugliest dogs she'd ever laid eyes on. Then again, all dogs were ugly to her. They...drooled all over you. And Caramel also seemed to have a gastrointestinal problem that no food the vet recommended solved.

It had taken her awhile to figure out that one. She'd suffered through countless noxious clouds before she'd finally determined the smell wasn't coming from a backed-up sink or a neighbor's garbage but was instead from the little dog that constantly panted at her feet.

"Can't you, please, please take her back to the ranch?" Dulcy was already shaking her head. "I just got her back from obedience school and she still doesn't have a clue that 'no' doesn't mean squatting on my bed.''

''Maybe because 'no' is the only word you're saying to her.''

Jena made a face as the phone at her elbow chirped. ''Ha ha. You, a comedian. Who would have guessed?''

''Lunch?'' Dulcy asked, getting up.

Jena reached for the receiver. ''Love to but I can't. Meeting with a client,'' she lied.

She answered the phone and began talking to the secretary of opposing counsel in a third case, not lifting her gaze again until Dulcy was on her way out the door. The instant her friend was gone, she put the caller on hold, then flopped back in her chair. She'd never lied to either Dulcy or Marie before. And to get out of a lunch that the firm would probably pick up...well, that was another first.

Yes, something was definitely wrong with her. And she wasn't all that sure she wanted to find out what.

No, she was positive she didn't. And she knew the one, surefire way to put it out of her mind. Continue on with business as usual—not only at work, but in her personal life.

Yes. That was it.

She punched the button to bring the caller back. ''So, Iris, what can I do you for?''

''THAT DOES IT. I NEED A wife.'' Jena stared into her empty refrigerator later that night, making a face at the container of half-eaten strawberry yogurt, the bottle of orange juice, and an unappealing container of Chinese takeout food. At her feet, Caramel looked from the refrigerator, to her, then back again, her tongue forever lolling out of her mouth. Jena asked her to move her tongue so she could close the refrigerator door.

"Hmm. I don't suppose you would know how one goes about getting a wife?"

Caramel tilted her head, either trying to understand what she was saying or else questioning her sanity. It had been a month since Dulcy had dropped the little fleabag off with detailed instructions on how to care for her—too bad it hadn't been an operating manual—and the number to a nearby vet.

Jena stared at the smelly canine. Okay, so she *was* cute. And she did make the apartment seem less... empty somehow. Not that she'd thought it empty to begin with. She only wished Dulcy had given her a later model that was already properly trained. Between arranging for a neighbor to walk the boxer, and rearranging her own familiar routine to accommodate the animal, she thought that having the pet came very close to having a child. She depended on Jena for everything every moment of the day. And that entire concept had scared the hell out of her.

But now that they'd both settled into a routine of sorts, it actually wasn't so bad. If Caramel would stop mauling Jena's favorite XOXO shoes, would pick a food she liked and didn't cause her to stink up the joint, life would be perfect.

Well, almost perfect. There was still the man matter. And the little problem of what she was going to eat tonight.

She went through her cupboards one by one. Empty cracker box. Dusty cans of lentil soup she couldn't remember buying. A jar of peanut butter that was useless without jelly, even if she had the bread to spread it on. And her large collection of art deco plates was completely useless without anything edible to put on them except dog food. Dog food, she had.

It was just after 7:00 p.m., dark as Hades outside, with absolutely nothing on television. And Jena was about to go crazy trying not to think about the realizations she'd come to with Mona and Dulcy's help earlier in the day.

Imagine, her without a man for three months.

She stilled, her hand in the process of closing one of the cupboards, and wondered why then she wasn't out on the prowl even now.

Pizza. So what if she'd had it twice so far this week? A nice, thick Sicilian from Mario's would do the trick right about now. And—who knew?—maybe the delivery boy would make her stop thinking about the sad state of her sex life.

Within moments she had her pizza ordered, poured

herself a glass of ever-present wine, fed Caramel a treat, then stepped into her large living room decorated in various shades of black, gray, red and white. There wasn't a single mid-western or Indian piece in the two-bedroom condo. Well, aside from the foot-high iron Kokopelli on the side table next to the lamp. But that had been a gift from Marie and she was required to display it, so that didn't count. Her tastes tended toward the more modern, citified look. She put her wineglass on the gray swirled marble coffee table, then picked up the remote control, flipping through the channels idly. Out of the corner of her eye she caught Caramel nosing in a flowerpot in the corner. The mutt had turned the plant over no fewer than ten times in four weeks. And, it seemed, obedience school had merely heightened the dog's interest in the forbidden plant.

"No!" Jena said, shaking her finger at the dog.

Caramel looked at her, her snout covered with dirt.

The doorbell echoed through the apartment.

Jena frowned at the dog, then glanced toward the door. Strange. The pizza place had never been this quick before. Sure, they were only five minutes away, but she didn't think even that amount of time had passed.

She tossed the remote to the couch, shooed Caramel away from the plant, then headed for the door.

But standing on the other side wasn't some post-adolescent teen with bad skin and braces, holding a pizza. Instead there in all his sexy glory stood the focus of her daydreams as of late: Tommy "Wild Man" Brodie.

Jena smiled so wide her face hurt. "How did you know you were just what I was looking to eat?"

ONLY MOMENTS BEFORE, Tommy's recovering knee had been throbbing, the pain made more acute by the thin chill of Albuquerque, his mood dark and grouchy. He'd been wondering what he'd been thinking, flying from L.A. on a whim, tired of sitting around his apartment by himself, sick of his own company, and not up to another round of smothering from his mother, albeit via the phone from Minnesota.

But as he stood looking at the woman he'd been thinking about nonstop for the past three months, his mood lightened, he forgot about his knee, and certain body parts that had been dormant since that one incredible night with Jena McCade sparked to life.

Hell, but she looked good. Damn good. Her shoulder-length black hair was slightly tousled as if she'd been running her fingers through it, her purple short, short nightgown shimmered in the light as she moved, and her violet eyes first looked large as hockey pucks, then squinted at him as she smiled that provocative smile he remembered so well.

"Get in here," her lush mouth said as she grabbed his arm and yanked him inside.

And in Tommy went, the door slamming closed

behind him, his duffel bag dropping to the ground as Jena practically launched herself into his arms. He automatically balanced his weight on his good knee as she wound her arms around his neck, then used them to pull herself up and straddle his hips, locking her bare feet behind his back.

Pain shot up Tommy's right knee, but he purposely ignored everything but the flames of craving licking through his bloodstream, filling him with a need for the woman even now launching a ravenous assault on his mouth.

Absently, he noticed the yapping of a dog. But he was too far gone to look around for it. Instead he groaned and curved his hands up Jena's legs then her bottom to support her. He wasn't surprised to find that she wore nothing under the slinky number. Her skin was hot under his fingers as he dipped his tongue into her mouth, his eyes watching her under half-closed lids.

She was even prettier than he remembered. Her angular features might have looked sharp on another woman, but they fit Jena to a T. She was as unpredictable as she was beautiful, and was the only woman up to this point in his life who had been able to match him stroke for stroke, lick for lick. In fact, in the twelve straight hours they'd spent together, she'd nearly undone him. Which was saying a lot considering his eight years on the professional hockey circuit spent sampling the willing fans and strangers alike offered up at every turn.

Jena finally paused for breath, resting her forehead against his as she laughed huskily.

Tommy slid his hands toward her slick flesh, stopping mere millimeters short. "Now that's what I call a welcome."

"I aim to please."

"I know."

She glanced over his shoulder at his duffel. "How long you in town for?"

He followed her gaze to find a blond boxer sniffing around the perimeter of the bag. "A couple of days."

Her provocative smile sent shivers down his spine. "That should do."

He chuckled as she unwound her legs from his hips and began to slide down. Her foot hit his knee brace.

"Here, let me help," he said, easily grasping her hips and putting her down on the floor.

"What's that?" she asked, feeling his brace through the loose denim of his jeans.

He shrugged, following the ends of her silky dark hair with a fingertip. "Let's just say I'm in need of some primo T.L.C."

She twisted her lips as she made a production out of looking him up and down. "I don't know how tender or loving it's going to be, but if it's a workout you're looking for…"

"That'll do."

"Good."

He grinned.

She took his hand and began leading him back, presumably to her bedroom. Halfway there, she halted. "Wait a minute."

"I don't know if I can."

"Well, you're going to have to, unless you want a devil on four legs drooping on your face while you sleep."

"Who said anything about sleeping."

"Oh, a man after my own heart."

Tommy sniffed. "What's that smell?"

"Don't ask."

He watched as Jena comically chased the puppy around the living room then finally nabbed her next to a large potted plant that teetered ominously. He'd never have guessed that Jena was a dog person. Then again, it appeared the role was a new one. He watched her lead the puppy to the kitchen as if the pup were the boss instead of her. She held up one finger to Tommy, then disappeared into the other room. The rustling of paper, the murmur of Jena speaking to the dog, then she was again in front of him, the kitchen door firmly shut.

She slid her tongue over her lips. "Now, where were we?" She smiled. "Ah, yes."

She took his hand again and picked up where she'd left off, namely en route to her bedroom.

He eyed her firm backside as she swayed her hips

in front of him. Oh, yeah. Exactly what the doctor ordered. Not his doctor, but the one lurking in the corner of his mind. The truth was, he'd missed this spitfire. Some would argue that he didn't even know her. He would tell them that he knew her better than he had any other woman in his life outside his mother and four older sisters.

But, of course, no one would argue anything with him, simply because no one knew about Jena McCade or the night they'd shared together. No one knew where he was now, either. They had the number to his cell phone. That was enough. And even that he'd turned off as the taxi had pulled up to the apartment building he'd found via a simple check of the phone book. He'd spent the past seven weeks going to physical therapy sessions and various sports doctors and he'd had enough of all of it. He didn't want to talk about his career and where it went from there, especially midseason and it was looking like he wouldn't make it back until next season, if then. This morning when he'd woken to the sound of his sports agent calling to remind him of his physical therapy session, all he could think of was getting out of L.A. And Jena was the first person who popped to mind. The person who had been on his mind constantly since before his injury during the game against the Detroit Red Wings seven weeks ago when he'd taken a stick to the skates and done the equivalent of an acrobatic twist a full fifteen feet in the air before landing in an inhuman position on the hard ice. Initially the dozen or so doctors the team had called in had wondered if he'd ever be able to walk on his shattered knee again, even after surgery. Their opinions reinforced the uncertain prognosis he'd given himself. Now...

Well, he didn't want to think about now in connection to his knee and what his own medical background told him might or might not happen. Not when Jena had entered the darkness of her bedroom and was tugging off her nightie, tousling her sexy hair all the more.

Oh, no, he didn't want to think of any of that. All he wanted to do was touch and be touched.

Jena tucked her fingers into the waist of his jeans and tugged him toward her.

And, oh boy, had he ever come to the right place to do that.

The injury he would survive. But as Jena kissed him again, he briefly wondered if he'd survive her...

2

_____

HOT AND SALTY AND one-hundred-percent male.
That's what Tommy's skin tasted like against Jena's
tongue. As the early morning sunlight slanted through
the vertical blinds cutting slashes of light across her
black lacquer bed, she slid a little closer to the man
sleeping next to her, allowing for a fuller taste of the
skin covering his broad shoulder.

Tommy made a sound deep in his throat, making
her smile. She felt so thoroughly…sexed. Every inch
of her sang and ached and longed for even more of
the man who had taken her again and again and again
through the night—with only one brief pizza break.
The scent of his sex, their sex, mingled together,
tightening the ball of desire accumulating in her belly
yet again and pebbling her nipples where they
brushed against the crisp hair of his arm.

She propped herself up on one elbow and gazed
down at the man who had occupied so much of her
thoughts over the past ninety days…and who now
blissfully occupied her bed. Everything about Tommy
''Wild Man'' Brodie was…manly to the nth degree.
Even in sleep, his features were strong and broad and

handsome, his skin tight and tanned despite his spending so many hours on the ice. An almost blond lock of hair, lighter than the brown of the rest of his hair, teased a thick dark brow. She reached up and brushed it back only to watch as it shifted back over his brow again. She sighed softly, wondering what he'd looked like as a boy. Had that shock of hair always been stubborn, no matter how often his mother tried to spit-comb it back?

Her gaze drifted down to his full, well-defined lips. Oh, what that decadent mouth was capable of. Just when she was determined to keep some secrets to herself, he'd fasten those lips around the core of her and give a little tug that made her open like a brand-new book eager to be read. His jaw was set even in sleep, and his Adam's apple bobbed as he swallowed.

Then there was that body…

Jena had dated many athletes in the past. She loved the solid feel of a man who looked after himself. The washboard abs. The hard muscles. At around six-foot three, Tommy's build was as solid and mouth-wateringly hard as they came. Each and every muscle was defined and honed and ready to touch. She lightly rasped the side of her hand down over a finely developed pec, over a dark nipple, then down the ripples of his abdomen and his waist to where the black top sheet was draped across his narrow hips. Then she slid her fingers under the soft material, seeking and instantly finding the long, thick ridge of his soft arousal underneath. She smiled as that softness transformed into a throbbing, steel-hard erection.

A low sound rumbled in Tommy's chest. "You didn't tell me you were such a pro at greetings."

Jena blinked up at him and smiled naughtily. "How do you mean?"

"Well, there was last night when I arrived. I don't think a man in the world could have asked for a, um, warmer welcome." His chocolate-brown eyes reflected amusement and heat as his right hand slipped down to cover her fingers, squeezing them against his flesh. "And if this isn't the best 'good morning' I've ever gotten, then it's a close second."

"I'll settle for best," she murmured, giving a squeeze of her own making.

She watched his throat work around a thick swallow. "Hmm."

She released him and folded back the sheet so she could get up.

"Whoa. Just where do you think you're going?"

She smiled over her bare shoulder. "To get ready for work."

He looked at her for a long moment, then his eyes narrowed. "We're going to have to work on your follow-up."

She laughed quietly and started to lift herself from the bed. He wrapped a hand around her wrist and hauled her back to him. She gasped. He grinned and waggled his brows at her.

"Surely you have five minutes."

"Not even two."

"Good, because one's all I need."

"Spoken like a true man." She laughed, wriggling against him, the crisp hair of his chest teasing her sensitive nipples. "Yes, well, I happen to need more."

"Think so, huh?"

"Know so."

His hands disappeared for a brief moment as he sheathed himself with one of the condoms he'd tossed to the bedside table the night before.

"Tommy…"

"Shh."

He rolled to his side then positioned her so that her bottom fit against him, snaking a hand around her hip and down to the V of her thighs. She gasped as he lightly pinched the flesh there then parted her to his attentions. In one smooth stroke he filled her from behind, pressing on her pulsing flesh from the front. Amazing even herself, Jena reached climax right then and there.

She fought to catch her breath even as he slowly rocked into her again.

"Told you," he whispered into her ear.

"Smart-ass."

He curved his fingers over her bottom. "Sweet ass."

She began to wriggle away.

''Where do you think you're going?''

''To shower.''

''I still have fifty-five seconds.''

Jena swallowed hard, the sensation of his thick flesh filling hers, the evidence of her own desire lubricating his strokes, heightening the chaos beginning to roll in her belly all over again.

''Oh, God,'' she murmured between clenched teeth.

''Oh, Tommy,'' he said in her ear.

Jena halted his fingers from where they tunneled in her curls then gave his hips a shove with her bottom until he was lying prone against the mattress. She followed, staying in the same position so that she straddled his hips with her back to him. Supporting herself with her hands between his legs, she moved up, then down, the length of his shaft, wishing she could see his expression, but getting immense satisfaction from the raspy sound of his breathing.

Up and down she moved, slowly, then more quickly, with each stroke stoking the flames licking through her body. Tommy grasped her hips, not halting her movements, rather enhancing them, his thumbs moving toward her bottom then parting her further.

His low groan sounded like he'd dredged it up from his chest. The sound wound around her, quickening her breath and her movements until skin slapped against skin, moans mingled with soft cries. Jena's muscles suddenly contracted so violently she froze. Tommy kept up the pace with his hands, pulling her down, then up, then down again, drawing out her crisis until he stiffened, thrusting deep inside her, joining her in the red cloud of sensation that had descended over her.

They stayed like that for long moments, neither of them in a hurry to emerge from the tranquil aftermath. Then Tommy slowly repositioned her until she lay flat against him, her back against his front, his arousal still filling her.

"I think you should call in sick," he murmured, absently stroking her breasts.

Jena nodded. "I think I should, too."

FOR TWO STRAIGHT DAYS Jena tried to escape the apartment. And for two straight days Tommy found inventive ways to stop her.

He leaned against the kitchen counter and crossed his jean-clad legs at the ankle, listening to the sound of the shower in the other room even as he stared at where Caramel had taken up residence at his feet. Did he dare try for a third day? He could climb into the shower with her as he had done yesterday, work her up into a lather in more ways than one...

He downed the rest of his orange juice then rinsed the glass in the sink. No. Jena was a shrewd one. She might get caught off guard once, but never twice by the same situation.

No, he'd have to come up with something else.

He caught himself grinning. Oh, yeah. Coming to Jena McCade's had been one of the smarter decisions he'd made in a while. Back in L.A. right now he'd be staring out at the Pacific outside his window, watching joggers with perfectly good legs eat up the beach and wondering just how in hell he'd gotten where he was. Yes, he knew. The problem was he'd begun to suspect his injury wasn't the only motivation behind the thought. Instead he'd begun to look at his life in a different light. Without the day-to-day busyness that went with being a hockey player, the workouts, the practices, the scrimmages, the games both on and off the road…well, he'd come to the conclusion that he had too much time on his hands.

Time Jena knew all too well what to do with. With Jena, he didn't have to think about whether or not he wanted to sit restlessly on the bench as the rest of his team played. Or worry that his knee might never feel the same again. He just…was.

And, oh, what a "was" it was, too.

Unfortunately it looked like that "was"…well, was coming to an end. Life was intruding with Jena going off to work. And, he reluctantly admitted, maybe it was time he let some of his own life back in. He'd known this brief interlude was meant to be brief. Yet he didn't want it to end just yet, whether Jena went to work or not. After all, she had to come home at some point, right? And when she did…

Caramel pulled him out of his reverie by making a sound at his feet. He considered the fur ball. The two of them had come to a truce early on. He didn't mess with her; she didn't mess with him. He could, however, do without the smell that seemed to accompany her presence.

He fished his cell phone out of his jeans pocket and reviewed his voice mail. Five messages from his agent. Two from his physical therapist's office. One from his mother. He chose his agent first.

"Jesus H. Christ, man, where have you been? I've been trying to get ahold of you forever. It's like you dropped off the edge of the Earth, Brodie."

Tommy rubbed his brow. Maybe calling Kostas Volanis back hadn't been the greatest idea. His time could be better spent coming up with ways to get Jena back into bed.

He envisioned her smooth, clean skin under the spray of the shower and his mouth watered.

"Tom?"

"I'm here."

"And where exactly is there?"

Tommy grinned. The question might appear innocent to others, but others didn't know Kostas the way he did. "Wouldn't you like to know?"

"Yeah, me and twelve other people. Hell, guy, you picked a helluva time to up and take off, you know? You've got the team owner wanting a status report on your rehab. Only the team doc said you didn't make your appointment yesterday. Then there is the sports equipment contract. You know they start shooting the commercials next month, don't you? That is, if you don't land on the permanently injured list. Did you take off back to Minnesota? You did, didn't you?'' He sighed. ''You're at least keeping off the knee, aren't you? Doing the exercises the therapist prescribed for you?''

''I'm taking care of it.'' Tom caught himself absently rubbing the knee in question and grimaced. Okay, so maybe he hadn't been looking after it as diligently as he should have, and given his own background in medicine, the sin was doubly inexcusable. He heard the hair dryer click on in the other room, dimming his chances of getting Jena to stay home again today. Okay, so maybe even he could do with a brief break from their bedroom activities. Bum knee aside, he swore muscles hurt that he hadn't known he had, fortifying his accredited knowledge that sex was one of the most strenuous physical workouts known to man.

''Look, Kostas, I've got to run.''

''Figuratively, right? You mean that figuratively. The doc said no running until—''

Tom chuckled. ''Figuratively.''

''So I call your parents if I need anything, right?''

Well, that explained the message from his mother. Likely mother hen Kostas had called Helen Brodie and made his disappearing act sound like a major event, which he supposed for all intents and purposes it was. He'd never taken off like this before without letting anyone know where he was. And given everything that had happened over the past couple of months, it was only natural that his agent and others would be concerned about him.

He just wished they'd stop.

"No, call my cell."

"So you're not in Minnesota then?"

"Talk to you later, Kostas."

"Wait, Tom—"

Tom clicked the phone shut then tucked it back into his pocket. He'd wait until later in the morning to call back the doctor's office and his mother.

The hair dryer switched off.

He grinned. Ah, Jena.

He hadn't quite known what to expect when he'd shown up three days before, but what he'd gotten had blown even that out of the water. He'd somehow forgotten how utterly hot she was. And he wasn't talking just in the looks department. Between the sheets, up against the wall, in the shower, Jena was thick, molten lava, metamorphosing to fit whatever role she had in mind.

Personally, he liked the wildcat the best. When Jena took charge, ordering him around, telling him to touch her just so, move like this, thrust like that, he was like a man gone insane. He hadn't let his injury hinder him in the least. Only problem was his knee was letting him know that now.

He opened the refrigerator door and stared at the slim pickings. Yesterday afternoon while she was napping he'd hit a nearby supermarket to stock up on the basics. Protein and complex carbs and plenty of them had been the order of the day. Plucking up the egg substitute carton and a package of turkey bacon, he turned toward the stove and started breakfast.

He didn't so much see Jena come into the kitchen as smell her. He breathed in the scent of her spicy perfume and said without looking, ''Good morning.''

''Bah humbug,'' she said, though her tone was lighter than the words implied. ''What, no coffee?''

''I don't drink it,'' he said. He turned, taking in the neat, sexy lines of her short skirt and business jacket. ''Neither have you for the past two days.'' He reached around where she was filling the coffeemaker with grounds and water. ''Try some OJ.''

''That, too.'' She switched on the maker then took the carton from him. Without breaking stride, she opened the top and drank straight from the carton.

Tommy lifted his brows and chuckled. ''You're kidding me, right?''

She shrugged and put the carton back in the fridge. ''Why dirty a glass?'' She smiled at him. ''See. I got my vitamin C and saved on the water bill. Environmentally friendly, me.''

Tommy gently grasped her by the shoulders and

pulled her to him. He wiped a drop of juice from the corner of her mouth. "Sloppy you."

She made a face and he kissed her.

"Hmm, citrus."

"Hmm, I'm late."

He chuckled and brushed his fingers through her silky hair, watching as the raven-black strands swayed back into place around her enchanting face. "What are the chances of talking you into staying home again today?"

Jena pretended to consider the question, then said, "Oh, I don't know. Between slim and none, maybe?"

He lowered his hands to her collarbone, pressing a thumb gently against her pulse point. He was rewarded with a small leap of her heartbeat. "Need I remind you that's what you said yesterday?" He placed a kiss to her temple then softly blew into the perfect shell of her ear. "And the day before that?"

He heard the click of her swallow. "Yes, well, I didn't have anything pressing on tap. Today…today, I have to go to the county jail to meet with a client."

"Hmm. Sounds ominous."

"Not if I get her out."

How was a guy supposed to compete with that?

As if of their own accord, his hands slid down her elegant back to her pert tush then brought her up against his growing arousal.

Behind her the coffeemaker stopped make spitting sounds. "Um, my joe's ready."

"Your joe isn't the only thing ready."

Her husky laugh heightened his desire along with the feel of her pressing against him. "Do you ever stop?"

"Do you want me to?"

She looked at him intently and he stared back. Her tongue ran the length of her lower lip. "Um, no."

But she did wriggle free from his grasp, then rifled through the cabinets and the dishwasher for an enormous travel cup. She filled the plastic to the rim with the coffee, then snapped on the lid. "Will you be here when I get back?" she asked, her back to him.

He noted the tension in her shoulders. He hadn't thought about it, really. He'd assumed he'd probably stay at her place, but hadn't considered her not being in it at the time. In fact, he hadn't given much thought one way or another regarding his trip to Albuquerque time wise, except that he'd eventually leave again. He'd merely hopped on a plane and was there an hour and a half later.

"Depends."

She turned toward him. "On what?"

"On whether or not you want me to be."

A shadow passed through her violet eyes. He grinned. Ah, a woman who liked to wield her power in bed but didn't want to call the shots outside of it.

That was okay with him.

She cleared her throat. "I don't know what bothers

me more. The thought of leaving you alone in my place, or your not being here when I get back.''

''Is that a yes or a no?''

She tilted her head slightly. ''You know, you never did say why you were in town. Is there, um, a game or something?''

''Or something.''

Her gaze drifted to his knee. ''There isn't, is there?''

''Are you asking me whether or not I came here to see you?''

She considered the question for a long moment. ''Yes, I am.''

''Then yes, I did.''

Her expression of surprise was the last thing he expected.

''When do you leave?''

''Depends.''

She twisted her lips, but didn't ask the question she had the last time he said the word. ''I've got to go. A girl will be stopping by every two hours to take Caramel out for a walk. She has her own key, but you may want to let her know you're here or she's liable to call 911.''

''Whoa,'' he said, catching her around the waist. ''At least have some breakfast.''

''I don't do breakfast.''

''Most important meal of the day, you know.''

She smiled. ''No, I didn't.''

Tom kissed her. Hard. Not releasing her until the question she hadn't asked vanished from her eyes and her body melded to his.

"You better get going," he said. "Someone's freedom hangs in the balance."

"Umm, freedom." Realization seeped back into her sexy eyes. "Oh, God, I am so late."

She started to pass him. He reached out and swatted her soundly on the bottom. She gasped then laughed, half turning as she made her way toward the door, Caramel nipping at her ankles. "I, um, guess I'll see you later then."

"Later."

She practically ran out the door, stopping before she closed it to grab her coat from a rack in the foyer. She shot him one last smile then disappeared, this time closing the door quickly to stop Caramel from getting out after her.

Tommy stood staring at the empty air for long moments, then shook his head. An enigma. Pure and simple.

Caramel's nails clicked on the floor as she gave up on Jena and the door and instead plopped down to consider Tom.

"Well, fleabag, looks like it's a table for two for breakfast."

3

JENA SLID HER CASE FILE into her briefcase and snapped the flap closed. In four short hours she'd accomplished more at work than she had in the past four weeks. She leaned back in her office chair and stretched her hands behind her neck, noting how good she felt. No, good was far too tame a word. Fantastic. Terrific. Well sexed. And even hungry for more of what Tommy "Wild Man" Brodie had to give.

She smiled and absently reached for the receiver. Would he answer if she called? She always left the volume up on her answering machine to screen out telemarketers. She could always ask him to pick up.

"How are you feeling?"

"Hmm?" Jena looked up to find her partner and one of her two best friends, Marie Bertelli, standing in the doorway.

"Feeling," Marie repeated, leaning against the jamb. "As in, how are you?"

"Fine, I'm fine." Why wouldn't she be?

Well, maybe because she'd called in sick the past two days, that's why.

She snapped upright, kicking herself for having forgotten that important little detail.

Marie had been the only one not in that morning to feed the cock-and-bull story about having come down with some sort of bug. Oh, she had come down with a bug all right, and his name was Tommy.

"Fine now, I mean," Jena clarified, taking her hand from the phone and squelching the desire to hear Tommy's deep, rumbling voice.

"Good." Marie tucked her red, curly hair behind her right ear, apparently buying the lie hook, line and sinker. And why wouldn't she?

Sometimes her friend could be so naive. Cute, a hell of an attorney, but incredibly naive. She supposed that's what happened when you were the youngest of a large family with three older brothers and old-fashioned Italian beliefs. The concept of deception between friends had yet to even register with her. Aside from Marie's two-year stint in the L.A. district attorney's office, she had lived at home all her life.

Jena prided herself on not envying anyone—except when it came to Marie. As much as her friend moaned and complained about her overprotective family, she never once noticed the way Jena sometimes sighed wistfully, wishing she'd had such a restrictive, loving upbringing. Well, she supposed she had known a bit of that. Until she irreversibly lost both her parents in one fell swoop of fate when she was ten.

"Jena?"

"Hmm?"

"Are you sure you're feeling okay? I mean, maybe you should take a half day."

Jena smiled at her friend's clueless comment and refused to think about how good the suggestion sounded. "I wish I could." Well, at least that much was true. She did wish she were at her apartment with Tommy exploring the rest of the Kama Sutra positions from the book she kept on her bedside table. "But I have to head out to the detention center this morning to visit Patsy Glendale."

"Ah. The make-you-or-break-you case."

Jena made a face. "No, no, no. It's the make-me case." She set her briefcase upright and got to her feet. "I'm going to get her off."

Marie gave an exaggerated shudder. "Please tell me you believe it was self-defense."

"Of course it was."

Marie shrugged. "It's just the way you said it. You know, 'Get her off.' Made it sound like it didn't matter one way or the other to you."

"In all honesty, it doesn't. Everyone is entitled to fair representation, Marie." She shrugged into her coat. "What would you have us do? Walk Patsy straight to the electric chair for accidentally killing her husband in self-defense?"

"Lethal injection room in New Mexico. And not if it wasn't premeditated."

"But if it was…"

"You said it wasn't."

"And you're not catching my point." Jena came to stand in front of her younger friend. If the memory of her own parents surfaced a little bit more every time she worked on the Glendale case, that was only natural, wasn't it? And if that same memory made her want to change the system, there was nothing wrong with that either. "Was there a reason why you stopped by? You know, other than to give me a lesson on morality?"

"Oh! Yes. I almost forgot." She tucked the hair at the other side of her face behind her left ear. "I wanted to ask if you'd co with me on the Fuller case."

"I thought Dulcy was going to do that."

"She was. But what with her new condition and all… Anyway, the court date is set at the same time as her due date and I'd really hate to get all the way there and have no backup."

Jena twisted her lips. "Depends."

She gave a secret smile, remembering when Tommy had used the highly suggestive word on her earlier that morning, and her own puzzling response to it.

"On what?"

"On whether you'll co with me on this case."

"The Glendale case? The case of the wealthy socialite who whacks her husband and screams years of emotional abuse as the reason that's in all the newspapers and smeared all over the television? Oh, no fair.''

Jena lifted a finger. ''On the condition that there'll be no more conversations like the one we just had questioning the client's innocence.'' She lowered her voice to a mutter. ''And no comments like the one you just made.''

''But…''

''Uh-uh. Those are my terms. You want me to co on the whistle-blower Fuller case, you have to do the Glendale case.''

Marie made a comic face at her. ''Oh, okay. Done.''

''Good.''

''You want to catch dinner tonight?'' Marie asked, leaning against the desk.

Jena paused, then continued through the door. ''Rain check. I already have other plans.''

''Ah. A guy.''

Jena smiled, thinking the word grossly inadequate. Tommy was a god. A king. The eighth wonder of the world. ''Yes. A guy.''

IT HAD BEEN A LONG, long time since Jena had indulged in a genuine midnight snack. She, Dulcy and Marie used to make a habit of getting together at least one night a week to pig out on everything their little ole hearts desired and OD on old videos, but they'd stopped that a few months ago. She slowed her chewing, realizing that had happened just after Dulcy had met Quinn.

Is that what happened when women fell in love? Did everything else in their lives come a distant second within a blink of an eye?

The thought bothered her, but for only a moment. Because, right now, sitting across her kitchen table from Tommy in her old sweats, her muscles stretched, her skin refreshed from the brisk walk they'd given Caramel, for the first time she almost understood why Dulcy had stopped participating in their weekly get-togethers.

She slid her foot under the table to stick her toe under the hem of Tommy's jeans, still hungry for him even though by all rights she should have had her fill. But when it came to Tommy...well, she was beginning to fear she'd never get enough of him. Caramel stopped her foot halfway there and she nudged the puppy out of the way.

"That pizza is two days old," Tommy said, his brown eyes sexy, his hair tousled and reminding her how they had spent the past few hours. "How can you eat it?"

Jena distantly eyed the fruit he'd peeled and cut into precise pieces on a plate. "That fruit's healthy. How can you eat that?"

She picked up the last of the nuked pizza, plucked a piece of pepperoni off the top, then leisurely stuffed the rest into her mouth, making loud sounds of enjoyment as she finished it off. Tommy swallowed hard as he watched her movements. Jena made sure to take extra care in sucking her fingers in a provocative way.

"So how'd it go today?" he asked, clearing his throat then putting two pieces of orange on her sauce-smeared plate.

Jena made a face as she fed some pepperoni to Caramel. "Where?" Was her voice a little raspy? "At work?"

"Didn't you say you had to visit a client in jail?"

Jena's shoulders instantly tensed. He would have to remind her of something she'd prefer not to think about just then. "Oh, that."

"You know, that pepperoni isn't going to help her, um, stomach problems any." He looked at her. "It didn't go well, I take it."

"No, it went okay." She moved the fruit out of the way to get at a gob of remaining cheese. "It's just that…I don't know. Do you ever feel like you know someone but have these awful flashes that you might not know them that well after all?"

"Never."

She poked him with her cold toe. "I'm serious."

"Sure. Everyone feels that way at one time or another, I guess." He slid a peach slice into his mouth and made the same sounds of pleasure she had made moments before. Jena watched as peach juice dripped down the side of his mouth over his chin and felt her own mouth water. Oh, how she wished she were that peach.

"Do you know this client?"

"Know her?" She tugged her gaze from his decadent mouth. "No. Not very well anyway. I know of her. Her family is old society. The Glendales were friends of my parents." Jena's throat tightened at what she might have given away in the simple sentence. "Anyway, about four months ago Patsy Glendale murdered her husband. And I agreed to take on her case."

"That's the woman all over the news?"

"It reached L.A.?" Jena perked up a bit. She knew the case was high profile in Albuquerque. Had the national media picked up on it?

Tommy pointed toward the living room. "I caught a bit of the news earlier."

Jena deflated. "Oh."

His chuckle made her think of everything but Patsy Glendale and murder. "Don't sound so disappointed."

She shrugged, uncomfortable with having been found out. "It's just that this case…it's one of those make-you-or-break-you cases, you know? The kind that puts you on the front page of the local newspaper. Garners attention." She wiped her hands on her napkin. "You can't pay for that kind of PR. And seeing as Dulcy, Marie and I are still finding our footing…well, we can use all the PR we can get."

"So murderers can beat a path to your door?"

"No, so high-paying clients can keep us out of the rain."

She sat back and watched him cut another peach, putting a slice on her plate alongside the orange pieces she had yet to touch. "Did she do it?" he asked.

Jena was reminded of her conversation with Marie earlier. "Yes."

She waited for his response. Only he didn't indicate one way or another what he thought of her pronouncement. He merely continued peeling the peach then cutting it into easy, precise pieces. "Premeditated?"

"You're up on your legal jargon."

"I watched the Simpson trial like every other American."

She cracked a smile. "No. Self-defense."

"Intriguing."

"Yes, I'd say that's the word that definitely applies in this situation." She didn't catch herself putting fruit in her mouth until she was already chewing it. She paused, grudgingly finding it good. She couldn't remember the last time she'd had fruit. The only thing that came close to qualifying were the lemons she'd sucked on after shots of tequila at Dulcy's bachelorette party. The night she met Tommy.

"My father used to cut fruit like that," Jena said. Her eyes widened at the casual reference.

Tommy smiled. "Only child?"

"How'd you guess?"

"You have that only-child air about you. You know, confident, self-sufficient, a loner."

"You mean selfish, greedy and arrogant."

"I didn't say that."

"No, I did."

He slowly chewed on a piece of peach and motioned toward the corner of the kitchen. Jena found Caramel had given up on the two of them and the hope of any more tasty tidbits and was circling around and around before finally plopping down on top of her dog bed with a long-suffering sigh.

"You know, she could do with a little discipline," Tommy said.

Jena stared at him. "She just got back from three days at obedience school."

"I said discipline. From you. Dogs like to know who's in charge. And from what I can tell so far, she's in control of you instead of the other way around."

Jena made a face. "I'll take your words under advisement."

He chuckled. "You know, I always wondered what it would be like to be an only child," Tommy said, drawing her gaze back to him. "I have four older sisters."

"I always wondered what it would be like to have siblings. Brothers. Sisters. Didn't matter."

"Living hell."

"Being an only child wasn't exactly heaven on earth," she said quietly. Especially when you lost both your parents at the same time and ended up alone.

"You said that in the past tense."

She realized she had. She shrugged, trying to adopt an air of nonchalance. In truth, she hadn't spoken about what had happened to her parents in so long, she'd forgotten the stories she used to come up with to explain their absence to strangers. Car accident. Plane crash. Anything that made the loss less painful, less real. Anything but the truth. Only Dulcy and Marie and a few others knew that. And not even they suspected that she needed to take on the Glendale case as a result of that truth. "Yeah. They died. A long time ago."

"Aunts? Uncles? Cousins?"

"One aunt. She moved to Washington State a few years ago." She shook her head to move her hair from her eyes. "You?"

"Both parents still alive and kicking. They live in the same house they bought thirty-five years ago. My four sisters are in various stages of engagement, marriage and divorce. All of them live within a mile of my parents in Minneapolis."

"How did you end up in L.A.?"

"They matched my price."

"Ah."

The corners of his eyes crinkled in a way she found irresistibly sexy. "Yeah, ah."

"Do you miss them? Your family, I mean."

"Sometimes. But I try to get home at least once a month. I was just back there for Thanksgiving."

"And the knee brace?"

He fell silent although his expression didn't change. "Injury, eight weeks ago. It put me out of commission."

"So you haven't played since then?" Jena asked, her brows rising.

"Nope."

She considered that. What would she do if something happened and she wasn't able to be a lawyer for two months? "How do you feel about that?" she asked quietly.

His grin made her curl her toes against the kitchen tile. "Like picking you up and continuing a nonverbal conversation in the bedroom."

Jena laughed. And it felt so good to do so that she continued doing it until she discovered that Tommy had stopped chuckling and was watching her through suspicious eyes.

"Careful or you're liable to give a guy a complex."

"A big jock like you?" Jena reached for her plate only to find she'd demolished the fruit he'd put on it. He held out another piece, but waved her hand away when she reached for it. She leaned forward and opened her mouth, waiting until he slowly put it inside. She drew her lips along the length, then took it full in along with his fingers. His gaze fastened on the movement, he slowly withdrew his hand. She took her time chewing, watching his face as he watched her. His eyes darkened. His jaw tensed. And a restless kind of energy seemed to emanate from him and reverberate off of her.

"A big jock like me still has an ego, you know," he murmured, blinking up into her eyes.

"Trust me, baby, you don't have a thing to worry about in that department."

His grin was just this side of completely wicked. "I know."

"Has anyone ever told you you're also bigheaded?"

"Depends on which head you're talking about."

She rolled her eyes to stare at the ceiling, but before she could make a jab about his adolescent remark, he was sweeping her off her feet and up into his arms. She automatically clung to his bare shoulders, feeling his broad, hard chest against her side.

"Now, how about I go and show you just how bigheaded I can be?"

"Sounds like an idea to me."

4

TOMMY STRETCHED LANGUIDLY across the empty bed, aware of the morning light filtering through his closed eyelids. How long had it been since he'd slept in? Right after his injury bed rest had been the order of the day, but by six every morning he'd been wide-awake, cruising through the news channels and absorbing every word in the newspapers and medical journals while eating the breakfast the visiting nurse delivered.

Now Tommy squinted at the bedside clock, surprised to find it half past nine. He picked up a note propped against the lamp. "See you at five" was scrawled in barely legible letters along with a capital J. He put the note back down then joined his hands behind his head and grinned.

Coming to Albuquerque to see Jena had been his best idea yet. No Greek-American sports agent who spoke a million miles a minute knocking down his door. No physical therapists telling him what he was doing was all wrong for his knee. No team owner telling him via the coach that they needed him back on the ice now. No one but him and Jena and the sexual playground they'd made out of her ultra-modern apartment.

He glanced around, having gotten used to his surroundings remarkably quickly. His own place in L.A. was done in pale woods with wood-framed furniture covered in overstuffed brightly colored pillows and cushions, the walls dotted with framed old movie posters. Bogart was a favorite of his, as was Spencer Tracy. And, of course, you couldn't go wrong with Paul Newman and Steve McQueen, although their posters were a little more recent. Growing up with the long winters in Minnesota, there seemed to be little more to do than go to the movies or play hockey. He'd preferred the matinees where they still showed the old films, while his sisters attended the new runs at night. And while he'd taken to hockey, Jamie, Sandie, Mandie and Lainie had trained as figure skaters.

He rubbed the stubble along his jaw and wondered what Jena had done at the same age.

He remembered her two friends from the bar. Childhood friends, Jena had said. The blonde—Dulcy, Jena had told him later—had looked like she'd needed some lightening up, while Marie…well, if he'd had a younger sister, he guessed she would have looked pretty much like her. Cute and hungry, appearing not to know what part of life to bite off first, and too scared to try.

But Jena… He couldn't quite figure her out. Which was likely the reason he was so drawn to her. So many people he could pigeonhole in two minutes flat. But he'd spent the past four days with Jena and still didn't have a clue what she was all about. A daring wildcat in bed, and remarkably bold during conversations, it wasn't until much later that he'd realized she hadn't revealed a bit of herself while she'd gotten him to tell her his life story.

Most guys probably wouldn't question her behavior. Hell, they'd likely celebrate it. What man wouldn't want a woman with apparently no past who wanted you and didn't have an agenda when she jumped into bed with you?

She'd said her parents had died....

Tommy dry-washed his face with his hands. Had she mentioned how they had died? Or how old she'd been at the time? If she had, he couldn't remember. He'd been too busy concentrating on her decadent mouth as she devoured first her pizza, then inadvertently inhaled the fruit he'd fed her. And, of course, he'd been busy answering the questions he was now afraid were meant to distract him.

He pushed up to sit, gingerly moving his leg over the side of the bed and doing a few stretches before standing on it. He checked the brace, then grabbed a pair of skivvies from his duffel before heading for the bathroom, intending to catch a shower before responding to the soft whining on the other side of the kitchen door. He had a good half hour before twelve-year-old Paula showed up to walk Caramel. Maybe he'd leave a note for her and see to the task himself. He could use exercise that didn't include a mattress. And perhaps the cold morning air could help clear his conflicting thoughts as far as the dog's mistress was concerned.

It didn't sit well with him, knowing that while Jena shared herself with him completely on a physical plane, emotionally she was as much of a mystery as she'd been when he met her. Perhaps even more so, because he was sure her block wasn't inadvertent but intentional. The mystery was fine for a one-night stand. The exchange of names wasn't really necessary in those cases, much less the details of one's childhood. But as the nights accumulated, no matter how much time separated the first from the second, their bond was deepening. Although, he suspected, not on an emotional level. Not for Jena.

And he didn't think it wise to explore that avenue just yet. Not knowing what he did—or didn't—about Jena.

As he stepped under the shower's hot spray and began to soap up with her spicy soap he suspected didn't come off a regular store shelf, he wondered about her personal life up until now. She was, what? Around the same age as him? Thirty or pretty near to that. Had she ever been married? Ever come close?

Of course, he hadn't told her that he had been married once. Very briefly. Back when he was still young and stupid enough to mistake lust for love. It was his first year on the circuit and one of the rink groupies who followed the team to as many as the games as they could had targeted him in her crosshairs. His career had been going like gangbusters at the same time. The new up-and-comer with a bright future. Landing the cover of *Sports Illustrated* hadn't hurt.

A month later they were married.

And a month after that he returned to their hotel room after a game in Toronto to find her in bed with one of the team's longtime heroes.

He shut off the water and scrubbed himself with a thick, black towel. The strange thing of it was that neither his ex-wife nor his fellow team member had seemed particularly shocked that he had found them. Rather, they'd been surprised that he'd cared that his friend was boinking his wife.

She'd argued that certainly he'd known of her goal to bed every major hockey star in the western hemisphere, hadn't he? The expensive rock on her finger hadn't changed that. And it was all right with her if he slept with groupies, she'd told him. He would anyway once the honeymoon was over.

The only thing that was over at that moment was their marriage—if there really had been a marriage to begin with.

He'd pretty much accepted life as it came after that. And had never really met anyone he wanted more than a quick roll in the hay with. Until Jena, that is.

But it was important that he get to know her if

this—whatever was happening between them—was to go any further. And he found he wanted that. Very much. Or else he would have left days ago.

The sound of the doorbell pealed through the apartment. Tommy slowed his movements and stared in the direction of the front door. Too early for Paula, but maybe she had something else on tap this morning and was getting an early start. Stepping out of the tub, he wrapped the towel around his midsection then strode to stare through the peephole. A deliveryman stood in the hall holding a package, about to ring the bell again.

"Yes?" he called.

He watched the man's gaze fix on the peephole. "Delivery for a Tommy Brodie."

Delivery? For him?

Damn, how had Kostas found him so quickly? He raked his fingers through his damp hair and unlocked and opened the door. As he signed for the package he heard footsteps on the staircase coming from upstairs. Paula bounded to a stop as Tom handed the deliveryman back his clipboard.

He waited until the guy started out before he told Paula, "I was thinking I'd look after the little mongrel today, give you a break."

Jena had introduced him to the preteen the morning after his arrival and since then the red-haired girl with braces had stared at him as if he walked on water. He grimaced. Hell, he'd settle for walking without a limp right now.

"Okay, Mr. Wild…I mean, Brodie."

Tommy grinned and handed her the money she would have made for the day's activities, then went back inside the apartment and closed the door, package in hand.

The return address was local. He frowned and ripped open the end as he walked to the kitchen and opened the swinging door with his shoulder, letting out the ecstatic pup.

His brows rose high on his forehead as he got an eyeful of the box's contents. A tux?

He stared at the monkey suit as if it might grow legs and challenge him to a choking match even as Caramel ran circles around his ankles, yipping up a storm.

Tommy shoved the suit back into the box, then ripped the envelope from the top.

"Formal Christmas party tonight," Jena wrote, along with an address. "Meet me there at six."

He took the suit out again and draped it over the back of a black leather chair, a slip of paper floating to the floor by his feet. He bent over and snatched it up. It wasn't a rental. Jena had dumped good money by buying the damn thing.

Tommy absently rubbed the back of his neck, trying to ease the tension building there. When was the last time he'd worn a tux? It didn't take him long to remember. He'd been nineteen at his oldest sister Jamie's wedding. And he'd completely ruined the rental by pulling and plucking and generally setting out to destroy the confining suit of clothes before it destroyed him.

He was not wearing that tux.

He eyed where Caramel was sniffing the edge of the stiff black fabric and had half a mind to give the dog a nudge until she grabbed it between her sharp little teeth.

The phone on the hall table began to ring. He stood staring at the tux as the answering machine picked up.

"Tommy?" Jena's voice came on after her short, sexy announcement. "Did you get the delivery yet?"

He strode to pick up the receiver. "Yeah, I got it."

"Good." She sounded satisfied. "Have you tried it on?"

"No." And if he had a brain in his head he wouldn't either.

Silence.

"It just arrived," he added.

"Oh. Good." There was the sound of another voice on her end of the line, then the chirp of a phone. "Look, I gotta run. I just wanted to make sure it got there all right."

"Oh, it got here all right."

"See you at six then?"

"Hmm. Six."

Tommy slowly replaced the receiver then stood there for long moments, wondering at the odd sensation settling over his skin. A kept man. That's what he felt like. A kept man waiting for his sugar momma—or whatever the female equivalent to a sugar daddy was—to come home to take care of him. A guy who sat around waiting to be told what to do. Wear this. Go here. Do that.

Wow.

Very definitely wow.

And very definitely no way.

He picked up the phone and dialed the number on the receipt in his hands, arranging to have the monkey suit picked up before he did something radical. Then he placed a call to information and asked for men's shops in the area.

Ten minutes later, fully dressed, a leash secured to Caramel's collar and his decision made, he felt much better.

And he knew that, starting now, things were going to start traveling in a different direction.

Either that or he'd have to head back to L.A.

No. That wasn't even an option.

"I HATE THESE THINGS."

Jena glanced at where Marie was plucking at the slinky straps of the dress she'd borrowed from Jena, misery written so thoroughly across her freckled face it nearly made her laugh. And almost made her forget about the fantasy she'd been entertaining and expanding on all night long. Namely her, Tommy, and a long ride in a luxurious, very private limousine that would have nothing to do with getting them where they were going.

"I always feel like I'm on display or something," Marie continued, shaking her foot, futilely trying to get her skirt to move down an inch or two.

"Would you stop fussing and smile?" Jena said with a smile of her own that was as much for her friend as a result of her continuing fantasy.

First, she'd straddle his lap. Next, she'd bare her breasts. Then—

"I'm not fussing."

Jena cleared her throat and at the same time, forced herself to clear her mind of the erotic images. "Yes, you are. And you look like a five-year-old on the verge of a tantrum."

Jena knew the surefire way to get a rise out of her friend was to compare her to being a child. Marie had always hated that she was four years younger than Jena and Dulcy. And while Jena didn't exactly like being on the receiving end of one of Marie's exasperated glares, it was a far sight better than watching her pick and pluck at the simple black dress as if she were allergic to it.

The annual Christmas gathering for Albuquerque law professionals moved around from year to year and included museums and art galleries among the venues. This year, however, Second Circuit Court Judge Betty Bullock had agreed to have the party at her considerable estate. Most thought it was because she had further political aspirations, perhaps even had her eye on the governor's mansion. Jena looked around the large new home built to look old with sweeping staircases and high ceilings and ornate woodwork. As far as mansions went, this one certainly didn't suck. She stared up at the frescoed ceiling depicting the Sandia Mountains at sunset and sighed. She'd love to live in a place like this.

Marie fidgeted next to her, awkwardly elbowing Jena in the side. Of course, Marie would probably just as soon burn the place down as live in it.

"Two miles from here children are hungry." Marie confirmed Jena's suspicions. "What a waste."

Jena rolled her eyes. "Is it too much to ask you to enjoy yourself this one time?"

Marie stared at her. "Yes." She pointed to her watch. "Twenty minutes and I'm out the door."

"Well, we'd better get hopping then, hadn't we? You know, considering that one of our partners already opted out so she could spend the evening with that completely hideous husband of hers."

Marie blinked at her. "Quinn is not hideous."

"Facetious, Marie. I was being facetious."

Jena drew to a stop in front of one of the largest rooms she'd ever seen in a personal residence. In fact, it was a ballroom with warm terra-cotta tile, a full grand piano in the corner, a small orchestra set up off to the side of that, and with tables of food and full bars set up every five feet along the outer walls.

The grand piano, especially, caused even more decadent ideas to skate through her mind. She twisted her lips. If only there weren't so many people in attendance.

But, of course, she'd also need Tommy's *presence* to get any of her fantasies off the ground. She scanned the crowd.

"Wow."

Jena enjoyed Marie's momentary awe at their surroundings, knowing that in about ten seconds flat she'd probably start calculating the cost of the one-night gathering and how many families the money could feed for a year.

Jena craned her neck. Speaking of completely hideous men, Tommy should be hiding out here somewhere in the sea of formal tuxedos and sleek couture holiday dresses.

"I'm going to get a drink," Marie said quietly.

Jena gently grasped her arm. "Just make sure you at least seek Barry out and say hello before you call a taxi."

Marie sighed. "I will, I will."

Jena released her friend and watched her approach the nearest bar. If her step hesitated as a man with rich copper-kissed brown hair and classic features approached, Jena decided it was probably because she didn't want to talk to him. Then she caught a glimpse of her friend's impish face. A flush slowly crept up her cheeks, and her eyes suddenly seemed overly bright. Jena looked at the man a little closer. Ian Kilborn, originally from the D.A.'s office, now flying solo in his own venture. And doing quite well if the media coverage was to be believed. And she had no reason to disbelieve it. Did Marie know him? It appeared that she did. Interesting…

A low, rumbling chuckle sent a shiver shimmying over every inch of her flesh, exposed or otherwise. Jena would recognize that sound anywhere. She turned her attention from where Marie was now quietly talking to Ian Kilborn and scanned the various groups in front of her. She smiled. There. To the right she spotted Tommy's tall head above a gathering of pretty young attorneys fresh out of law school.

She breathed a silent sigh of relief. He'd made it.

She tucked her clutch purse under her arm and began making her way toward him, a weightless sensation taking root in her stomach as she anticipated putting her limo fantasy into play. The girls parted slightly and she looked down to see how the tux she'd bought looked on his glorious body. Her step faltered when she found he wasn't wearing a tuxedo at all, but rather dark slacks and a sleek stylish jacket over a black T-shirt. Okay, maybe it wasn't a T-shirt, T-shirt but it might as well have been given that every other man in the room wore a tux.

"Ah, and here she is now...."

Jena blinked to find Tommy addressing her. The women slowly stepped aside, putting her face-to-face with the man who had virtually taken her captive in her own apartment—a position the women around him appeared interested in applying for.

Tommy's grin did funny little things to even her toes. Sex, pure and simple, she told herself. "These lovely young ladies were questioning whether I was crashing the joint, or if I really was waiting for a date."

Jena smiled at the small group. Some she knew, others she was acquainted with, and one of them she'd only heard of. "Wishful thinking, perhaps?"

"Tommy was just telling us he could fit two of us in the Stanley Cup."

"Hmm...was he now?"

Tommy's expression grew curious as he watched her. "Yes, you know, the top hockey trophy?"

"I know what the Stanley Cup is," she said.

Jena wanted to stomp her foot, hard. Not because it was obvious that Tommy was as skillful a flirt as she was. She'd already known that. But because jealously had just reared its ugly little head and she felt like pointing to the exit and telling the young interns the door was that way and that they should leave if they ever hoped to get into a decent law firm.

"Excuse me, ladies," Tommy said, stepping through the middle of them and offering his arm to

Jena. "But I have something...of a personal nature to discuss with my date."

Titters and raunchy giggles followed in their wake as Tommy led Jena away from the small gathering. Uneasily, she realized that it wasn't so long ago that she would have been one of that group making comments on an attractive man, perhaps singling him out and trying to seduce him. The discovery didn't make her feel very good. In fact, it made her feel a bit on the cheap side. Definitely a new emotion to her, a woman who had always wholeheartedly believed that all was fair in the arena of love and war.

She stuck her chin up in the air, not about to let Tommy in on her thoughts. And not about to allow him to appease her so easily either. If he hoped to win her back over he was going to have to do some quick thinking.

She smiled knowingly to herself. If anyone was capable of quick thinking and inventive maneuvers, Tommy was. She shivered as she waited to see what he had in mind this time. And how her own secret little plan might throw him for a loop....

5

I'LL BE DAMNED. She's jealous.

Tommy rubbed his chin, trying to contain his grin. Oh, he was well versed on the concept of jealousy. Not only because he'd seen the green-eyed monster in others, but because he'd felt the ugly emotion a time or two himself. And jealousy very clearly glittered in Jena's beautiful violet eyes.

They finally reached the fringe of the room well away from curious ears and he had to force himself to release her arm.

"You're not wearing the tux," she whispered as he picked up a champagne flute from a passing waiter and handed it to her.

"Nope."

"Didn't it fit?"

He shrugged nonchalantly. "I don't know."

"What do you mean you don't know? Didn't you try it on?"

Tommy met Jena's gaze straight on. "I don't do monkey suits, Jena."

She made face that was part exasperation, part disappointment. "Well, you could have told me that."

He cleared his throat as she took a slow sip of champagne. He licked his lips and realized he wished it were her lips he was licking. "And you could have asked."

They stared at each other for a long moment, then Jena's luscious mouth curved into a smile as if just getting a joke. Tommy chuckled.

She leaned closer to him, her breast brushing against his sleeve. "You know, I would have at least liked to have seen what you looked like in it."

He gestured toward the other men milling about the room. "Doesn't take much imagination. I'd look the same way the rest of these stiffs do."

Her eyes darkened as she gave him a lazy once-over. "Oh, no. You wouldn't resemble a single person here."

He puffed out his chest. "That's what I figured. So why try?"

Her naughty laugh made his collar feel tight around his neck even without one of those starchy ties. "Nice suit," she said.

He grinned. "Thanks."

"What did you do with the tux?"

"I let Caramel have it."

She nearly choked on the champagne she was drinking.

"I sent it back, of course," he said.

"I see."

Tommy eyed her steadily. He hoped she did see.

Truly saw. Because he was a man who prided himself on making his own decisions. Throughout his life he'd rebelled against how his mother tried to dress him, took back what his sisters bought for him. He'd never wanted to be a woman's version of a man. A guy taken to wearing pink sweaters because the women in his life thought it looked sexy when it really looked…gay. Purchased stuff for him that would look better on a woman.

No, he didn't go in for any of that. A slippery slope, that one. You gave in on one issue, and pretty soon the woman in your life was making every decision for you. Just like his mother made all the decisions for his father. And his sisters for their lovers and husbands.

Oh, no, definitely not a path that interested him. He was a man's man. And he liked his life just fine the way it was, thank you very much.

Tommy rubbed the back of his neck, experiencing a moment of pause. Unfortunately he wasn't all that clear on what did constitute his life at the moment.

Now that was a thought.

Okay, so he was a hockey player robbed of his stick because of a knee injury. He had an agent who left ten messages on his voice mail a day. And then there were his mother and sisters who had all stopped asking just when he was going to settle down, but the question lingered in their voices anyway.

So where did that leave him aside from in Albuquerque in a new suit at a Christmas party with Jena?

Tommy knocked back the champagne in his glass and smiled at Jena's questioning gaze.

Okay, so maybe his life was pretty much up in the air right now. But the path Jena had tried to point him down by sending him that tux didn't interest him. He didn't have what it took to be a kept man. He'd always bucked taking the easy route. It's what made him such a damn good hockey player. And, he hoped, a better man.

"Ladies and gentlemen, can I have your attention, please?" A woman's voice sounded from the far corner of the room near the gleaming grand piano as she tapped a spoon against a crystal glass.

"Our host," Jena whispered into his ear, "Judge Betty Bullock."

Tommy looked down to find her standing as close as physically possible while still wearing clothes and resisted the urge to breathe deeply of her spicy, musky scent. She wore a sexy red number that contrasted boldly with her silky black hair. Definitely not what she'd worn to work that morning. Either she had a full wardrobe at work, or she'd gone shopping during lunch. He suspected his second guess was more on target.

"Thank you all for coming to our, um, intimate gathering," their host continued, getting a few laughs from the large audience. "I thought it the perfect opportunity for us to get to know each other better. And what finer way to do that than to sing Christmas carols together?''

First groans then chuckles made the rounds around the room, Jena's the loudest. But Tommy was only vaguely paying attention. His mind wasn't on Jena's groan but rather on the heat that increased his own body temperature from merely standing next to her.

Their host continued, ''Bet you didn't know I played the piano, did you? So, if you don't mind humoring me, I'd like to play a couple of my personal favorites...''

Tommy could think of a couple of personal things he'd like to do, and neither of them included Christmas carols or crowded parties. He reached out and slid his hand into the spaghetti strap of Jena's dress and drew it so the back of his fingers skimmed her skin. She visibly shivered. She looked away from their host and up at him, her eyes wide and moist and giving him a message that she was ready for anything.

The judge took a seat behind the piano and slowly began a piece from the Nutcracker. The crowd was silent and attentive, but Tommy thought that could be as much out of boredom as genuine interest in the music.

He leaned down to whisper into Jena's ear. ''How long do we have to stay here?''

He watched her elegant throat work around a swallow. ''Why?''

"Because there's something else I'd much rather be doing right now."

"Oh?" she asked, her lips turning up into a saucy little smile. "What's that?"

Though he already suspected she knew exactly what, Tommy leaned over and proceeded to tell her, watching as her lips parted, her skin grew flushed and her breath caught.

Satisfied he'd gotten the desired result, he pulled back and grinned.

"Sounds tempting," she said, her voice dropping to that husky whisper that made his blood speed through his veins like a puck looking for the net.

He hiked a brow. "Merely tempting?"

"Mmm."

"Well, how about I add this…"

He leaned down and whispered into her ear again, taking his verbal seduction a step further and watching as her nipples bunched and pressed against the thin fabric of her dress as if aching to be freed. Her tongue darted out and moistened her bottom lip. He'd grown semihard the instant he spotted her in the room. Now his erection pulsed under the loose material of his slacks and was a heartbeat away from becoming obvious to anyone looking in their general direction.

Jena's breath exited in a soft gasp. She quietly cleared her throat. "And where, exactly, do you propose we do all, um, that?" she asked, the black of her pupils nearly obliterating all color in her irises.

"That depends."

"Ah. Conditions."

"Uh-huh."

She looked around the room. No one stood within hearing distance. "And those would be?"

"Oh, there's just one."

Her brows lifted fractionally. "Simple enough. What is it?"

He gave her a wicked grin. "That you do whatever I say when I say to do it."

She didn't say anything for a long moment, either because she didn't know what to say or because she was momentarily robbed of breath. "Dangerous position, that."

"Very."

She gazed around the room. Everyone's attention was on their host who had moved on to a more popular piece. A few of the guests even started singing along to…was that "Santa Claus is Coming To Town"?

"So are you up for the challenge?" he asked Jena, tucking her hand into the crook of his arm.

She tilted her head forward, looking at him from under the fringe of her dark lashes. "What are you planning to do? Borrow one of the bedrooms?"

Certainly she didn't think him as unimaginative as

all that? "You'll have to just wait and see, won't you?"

"Okay." The one word response came out as a half whisper, half whimper, the verbal interplay apparently having already made her hot.

He released his grip.

"Where are you going?"

"Shh," he said, pressing his finger against her luscious lips. "It will look suspicious if we both leave together."

"I see."

"I'm going to be around the corner in the hall. Wait a couple minutes, then follow me out."

She nodded just enough for him to see. He placed his glass of champagne on a nearby table, straightened his suit jacket, then strode from the room without a second glance.

It took every ounce of self-restraint Jena possessed not to follow Tommy out of the ballroom the instant he turned to leave. A waiter passed by and she placed her champagne flute on his empty tray, barely recognizing his expression of interest. On any other night she might have given the great-looking guy a second look. But not tonight. Tonight she had one man on her mind. And she barely had room in her mind to contain him.

Four days had passed since she'd found Tommy sitting on her doorstep like a tasty morsel just waiting to be devoured. But rather than getting her fill of him, every moment that passed increased the risk of that same desire overwhelming her entirely. A new emotion for her. And a dangerously exciting one. What scared her most was that she wasn't sure she could control the emotion if she were to try. And she definitely was not trying. The truth was, she liked the feeling of flying without a net. Of pushing off that cliff and trusting that she would be okay, even when she wasn't entirely certain that she would be.

Heat curled through her veins, making her almost unbearably hot as the judge finished one carol and launched into another lively tune. More of the guests had begun to join in, making Jena's escape even easier.

She briefly closed her eyes. This was crazy. Insane.

And she wanted to do it more than anything else in the world in that one moment.

Moving her clutch purse from one arm to the other, she fussed with her hair then headed for the door to the hall as if on her way to the bathroom to see to repairs. She casually glanced both ways then headed down the hall toward the back of the house, her heels clicking on the white and black marble tile. She rounded the corner, then gasped when Tommy hauled her first into his arms, then pushed her against the cool wall in the deserted secondary hallway.

"You took your sweet time getting here," he

rasped, eyeing her mouth in that predatory way that made her blood boil.

"I wanted to make sure no one followed me," she said, surprised at the shallowness of her breathing, the unbearable craving deep in her belly. He hadn't even touched her yet and she was afraid she was a heartbeat away from climax.

She watched as he slid his finger under one of her dress straps and tugged it down her bare arm until the fabric pulled tight against her breasts. He skimmed the same finger down and under the front of the dress. When it scraped against her hypersensitive, distended nipple she let out a small cry.

"Shh," he said, tipping his head forward and kissing her deeply. "We wouldn't want anyone to hear you and come investigate."

Jena gazed into his handsome face. "You're not suggesting…we're not going to…I don't think…"

"Oh, yes, we very definitely are." He licked her bottom lip then pulled it into his mouth. "Don't think, Jena. Just feel."

She arched her neck as wild abandon shot through her. Oh, she was definitely feeling. And all thought of getting him out to the waiting limousine flew completely out the window. She was dying to see exactly what he had in mind right here, right now.

He maneuvered his finger under her breast and they both watched as the swollen crest popped up and out of the fabric, her skin pale against the deep scarlet of the fabric. Tommy made a small sound in his throat as he urgently reached down and bunched the skirt of her dress around her thighs then clutched her hips, nudging her up the wall until she was forced to curve her legs around him to keep her balance.

"Tommy!" she whispered harshly, her breathing ragged, her heart pounding almost painfully in her chest.

His hands swept behind her then down, tunneling into her panties and squeezing her bottom as he opened her to him.

His gaze slammed into hers, his deep brown eyes filled with sexy intent as he slanted his mouth over hers and drank deeply, demanding an equal response from her. Jena laced her hands behind his neck, the rough material of his jacket rubbing against her exposed breast, his fingers delving into her shallow crevice from behind and skillfully stroking her slick flesh, making her wetter yet.

"Oh, God," she whispered.

As adventurous as she was, Jena had never indulged her sexual appetite in a public place. Had never risked discovery by others. And the mere prospect that one of the well-groomed guests from the other room could round that corner at any moment further fuelled the flames licking over her skin until she nearly exploded.

Tommy navigated through her shallow fleshy crevice then thumbed the tight bud at her core. Jena held on for dear life and clamped her teeth together to cage the moan that threatened.

"You're so hot," Tommy whispered against the shell of her ear. He pinched her vulnerable flesh. "Are you hot for me, Jena?"

She looked from one of his eyes to the other. "You have no idea."

Tommy pressed his forehead against hers, holding her gaze as he slid a finger inside her dripping wetness. She gasped. "Oh, I think I do."

Bold need surged through Jena. She moved her hands from behind his neck, forcing the responsibility of balancing them on him alone as she fumbled between the lapels of his jacket for the front of his belt. She made quick work of it and within moments held his long, pulsing thickness in her hand.

"Mmm. Looks like I'm not the only one who's hot."

She squeezed her fingers around the hard flesh. He threw his head back and groaned, the sound mingling with the muted sounds of the piano in the other room.

Tommy freed one of his hands and within a blink had sheathed himself with a condom. Jena grasped his shoulders and positioned herself for easy access. Tommy didn't disappoint as he pushed aside her panties then filled her to the hilt.

Jena's breath caught and held in her lungs as every muscle clenched, pulled, tightened. A sweet weightlessness accumulated in her stomach, growing, twisting, surging. Tommy slid his hands up her bare legs to grasp her bottom, holding her steady as he rocked into her again.

"You drive me so crazy I can't think," he whispered between clenched teeth.

Jena barely registered the flattering comment as he thrust again, parting her with his hands from behind to allow for an even deeper meeting. He bent to pull her exposed nipple into his mouth and the sensation of weightlessness exploded into overwhelming pleasure. Tommy covered her mouth with his to trap her low moan even as he stroked her with his tongue and his erection. For long, unbearable moments Jena seemed to hover somewhere near the ceiling, suspended on a wave of impossible sensation. Then she finally collapsed, little more than a rag doll in his arms as he grinned down at her.

"Do you have any idea how incredibly beautiful you look when you're climaxing?" he asked.

Jena told herself she should be concerned about her appearance. The slight sheen of sweat that covered her skin. The condition of her mussed hair. But all she could do was smile back at him.

Then he rocked into her again and she gasped, aftershocks quaking through her.

"Did you think I was done?" he asked.

For the first time Jena looked beyond him to the hallway. There were two closed doors to her left, the main hall was around the corner to her right, and another closed door was down the hall. She was amazed they hadn't been caught yet. Then again, for all she knew, someone had come around the corner then backed away to give them privacy.

But how long would their luck hold out?

Tommy almost completely withdrew then surged up into her again, filling her to overflowing, chasing all care about their surroundings from her mind. She stretched her neck and tried to swallow the low cry that threatened, then tightened her legs around him, by extension tightening the muscles cradling his thick, hard erection.

She knew the instant his crisis loomed. He bucked boldly into her, his head back, a vein pulsing thickly in his neck, his hands grasping her bottom to the point of pain, holding her still, holding her tight against him. Merely watching him in the throes of passion, and knowing she was the cause of it, toppled her right over the edge with him, leaving no one on guard as a low moan ripped from her throat.

For long moments they stayed like that, still, their breathing labored, their hands clutching. Then slowly Tommy kissed her, igniting something warm in the pit of her chest.

"Have I told you how incredible you are?" he murmured, nipping at her neck.

Jena smiled languidly. "No. But I'm all for it."

He chuckled softly as he put her feet back down on the floor. Her skirt instantly settled back around her ankles as she bent to pick up her purse from the floor then handed him a tissue. He quickly took care of business and within moments they'd returned to the physical state they'd been in before they snuck out of the room.

Well, almost.

Jena brushed her fingers through Tommy's thick brown hair, toying with the splash of blond in the front that fell over his brow.

"What's say we get out of here?" Tommy asked.

Jena raised a brow. "Why? I kind of like the thought of going back in there and mingling a bit knowing we just had sex out here in the hall."

He tapped his finger against her nose. "You're a naughty, naughty girl, Jena."

"And you're a wicked man."

He chuckled and began leading them around the corner where they bumped into a man coming from the opposite direction.

"Pardon me," an old associate attorney of Jena's said.

"Excuse me," Tommy said.

They navigated around each other, then Jena dissolved into a series of uncontrollable giggles.

"On the other hand, I think your idea is the better one," she said once she had finally gotten control of herself. "Let's get out of here."

6

"WHO WAS THAT HOTTIE I saw you with last night?"
Marie asked.

Jena accepted her purse back from the guard at the
Bernalillo County Metropolitan Detention Center,
then gave her friend a long look. Of course, Marie
would choose now to ask the question, right before
they were to go in to visit her client, Patsy Glendale.
She couldn't have posed the question on the sixteen-
mile ride west out to the county jail. Or even back at
the office where they had commandeered one of the
conference rooms and spent the morning going over
the depositions piling up in the complicated case.

Jena smiled at the guard then Marie, stomping
down her immediate physical response that went
along with thoughts of Tommy. "Tell me why you
looked at Ian Kilborn as if you'd like to order him
up for dessert and I'll answer your question."

Marie's blue eyes widened. "I did not look at Ian
Kilborn in any such way."

Jena shook her finger as they followed another
guard through a reinforced metal door in the new fa-
cility and down a long hall to one of the attorney-

client meeting rooms where Patsy would be waiting for them. "Tsk tsk. You should know better than to try to deny things of that nature with me, Marie."

"I'm not denying anything. Something actually has to happen in order to deny it. We merely said hi, you know, the usual thing you say to an acquaintance when you run into each other."

"Uh-huh."

"Okay, so maybe it's more than that. After all, we all grew up in the same neighborhood." She stared at Jena. "Or don't you remember?"

Jena made a face, trying to think back to when they all were younger. Her eyes widened. "No! Not the tall, skinny guy with the perpetual sunburn that lived two blocks nearer the school?"

Marie grimaced.

"No wonder I didn't remember him." Jena stared blindly in front of her. "God, had I known he would turn into such a hunk, I would have been nicer to him."

Marie elbowed her. "You can be crass, you know?"

"So you keep telling me."

"Yes, well, let's hope one of these days my words sink in and you start believing me."

Jena laughed. "Then who would you go to for a good laugh?"

"Good point."

The guard unlocked the door to the meeting

room—a colorful improvement on the rooms of old but still little more than a ten-by-ten room with a bolted-down metal table and four chairs with a single lightbulb hanging from the ceiling. Jena's good humor vanished. She always hated visiting these places, no matter how new or how freshly painted. Aside from the instant sense of claustrophobia she experienced, the room depressed her, made her feel like a caged animal when she hadn't done anything wrong.

Marie lowered her voice. "You never answered my question, you know."

Jena flashed her a smile. "I know." She entered the room. "Hi, Patsy."

After an initial exchange of "how are yous" that seemed hollow given their surroundings—how else would Patsy Glendale be doing in the depressing place but badly?—the conversation switched completely to business. Marie fidgeted next to her, looking over her shoulder at the guard visible behind the twelve-by-twelve-inch mesh window of the door, then around the room as if afraid the walls might be closing in, while Jena brought Patsy up to date on the status of the case.

Handcuffs clinked as Patsy lifted her hands to rest on the table between them. "Has there been any progress on releasing me on bail?"

Jena stared at the cuffs, such inappropriate jewelry for a veteran socialite. In her early fifties, Patricia Lynn Glendale looked every minute of her age in that one moment. Stripped of her Estée Lauder makeup, her $150-an-hour hairstylist and her pricey clothing, she came across as any other woman might in the same position. All social and cultural lines erased.

Except for her posture. Even in the prison jumpsuit, Patsy managed to look…regal somehow. She'd probably spent months walking with a book on her head and a yardstick tied to her back when she was a teenager and it showed.

Not that it did her any good where she was now.

"No, I'm sorry," Jena said, finally answering her question. "Judge Madison refuses to reconsider." Jena tucked her hair behind her ear. "But I did talk to him about the problems you've been having with your cellmate and he agreed to have you moved to your own cell."

Marie stared at her. Yes, the allowance was unusual. But Jena had made the judge—an old family friend of the Glendales—feel so guilty about keeping her in custody until trial that he'd grudgingly agreed to her demand.

It didn't hurt that she'd made the situation seem much worse than what Patsy had complained about: her cellmate's atrocious language and nonexistent housekeeping habits.

Patsy briefly closed her eyes as if having been granted a huge favor. "Thank you."

"Just doing what you're paying me for." Jena looked through her files, avoiding doing what she'd come here to do. Marie cleared her throat. Jena purposefully ignored her.

"Ms. Glendale," Marie said, taking the initiative, "I'm sure you're wondering about the real reason behind my and Jena's request to see you today."

Patsy's eyes narrowed slightly as she looked at Marie. Jena gave a mental sigh. A bull in a china shop. That was Marie Bertelli. As sweet as chocolate when it came to personal relationships, she was all about cutting to the chase on the job. Jena figured much of it came from her stint in the L.A. district attorney's office. But she also knew that her no-nonsense family environment was also to credit…or to blame, considering the circumstances. If any of the Bertellis wanted to know anything, they asked. No two ways about it. With no regard about whether or not you wanted to be asked.

Marie didn't understand that sometimes a little finesse was called for. Patsy Glendale's case reeked of politics, as did Patsy herself.

Jena smiled at Patsy. "You'll have to excuse my partner," she said smoothly, "this is her first time out on a case of such importance."

Marie's brows rose almost up to her red hairline.

"Anyway, although her methods are a little…rough, Marie's right, Patsy. There's been a development we need to discuss with you."

"Development?"

"Yes. You see, the prosecutor has dug up a waitress from a restaurant—Georgio's, I think—who claims she overheard you talking to one of your friends during lunch about killing Harrison and making it look like self-defense.''

Jena kept her gaze steady on her client. Patsy didn't even blink. Merely stared at her as if they were discussing the time of day.

Marie cleared her throat. ''You can see where this could cause some problems.''

''Certainly this…service worker isn't being taken seriously?'' Patsy said.

''And why wouldn't she be?'' Marie asked.

''Because she's a service worker who likely makes minimum wage and is solely looking to improve her unfortunate social status.''

Jena turned the page in her notebook. ''It turns out Krista Denoto is the niece of the restaurant owner and is in graduate school with a guaranteed position at IBM headquarters when she graduates next spring.''

''No easy motive for lying,'' Marie pointed out, ''and very credible.''

Patsy kept her gaze on Jena.

''Of course,'' Jena said, ''the testimony is hearsay and I fully expect the judge to exclude it. But the prosecutor intends to pursue the matter until all avenues are exhausted. And until the jury has heard enough to tarnish your case.''

''From a service worker?''

"From a young woman who believes she's doing the right thing," Marie said firmly.

"Then, of course, there's the friend you were dining with…" Jena began.

Patsy raised her brows.

"They have yet to ascertain with whom you were dining since the reservation was in your name, but if you could provide the information we could possibly stop the prosecutor dead before we get to the courtroom in two weeks. If we can get a deposition from the friend you dined with disputing Ms. Denoto's testimony in her deposition, then the two would cancel each other out and the whole matter wouldn't make it into the courtroom."

Patsy pretended to consider her nails. "I dine at Georgio's often with several friends. It's impossible to know who the service worker is referring to."

Jena named a date some thirty days before the night Patsy killed her husband. "Certainly you could refer to your calendar or direct your social secretary to give me the information."

"I can't imagine what this witness claims to have heard," Patsy said, then sighed, her thoughts appearing to turn inward.

Jena tucked her hair behind her ear. "Likely it's something we all say without thinking at one time or another. You know, along the lines of 'I swear one of these days I'm going to kill him for leaving the top off the toothpaste.'"

Marie stared at her. "The deposition indicated words more serious than that."

Patsy looked at Jena.

Jena reluctantly admitted, "Unfortunately, Marie's right. The witness claims you were discussing the advantages of killing your husband over divorcing him."

"Why, that's preposterous. I can't imagine even thinking such thoughts much less discussing them with someone in a public venue."

"It was a private table in a restaurant," Marie pointed out.

"It never happened," Patsy maintained. She looked at Jena again. "I'll have my social secretary give you everything you ask for."

Jena nodded. "Good. That's what I was looking for." She started to put her materials back into her briefcase. "The guards are going through the things you requested now. I trust they'll be delivered to your cell later."

"Very good. Thank you."

"MARIE THINKS SHE'S guilty as hell."

Not exactly the conversation Tommy was aiming for. He slowed his hands where he was giving Jena a long, sensuous back rub in her dimly lit bedroom. It was after midnight and she'd just gotten home a short time ago looking exhausted and in need of everything but sex. He fed her first, under protest that she didn't like vegetarian lasagna. She'd gobbled it down though, like it was her favorite dish, while filling him in on her day. He knew what putting in a long day was like when he'd juggled hockey with a full university course load, or when the team played doubleheaders that left him drained and in need of nothing but a good meal and a soft bed.

He skillfully dug his fingers into her shoulder muscles and she stiffened, then relaxed again with a low moan. He said, "I thought it was already established that she did it."

"It was. I mean is." Jena turned her head to lie against the mattress, her lashes shadowing her cheeks, her silky hair settling immediately back into place. She wore nothing but the naughty purple chemise and panties she'd had on under her suit. "But Marie doesn't think self-defense played a role."

"And if it didn't?"

Jena was quiet.

"Interesting."

"What?"

Tommy lifted a brow at Jena's slightly defensive tone. "Nothing. I just thought your not answering my question was interesting, that's all."

She wriggled, suddenly restless between his legs, forcing him to climb off. He stretched out on his back beside her and entwined his fingers behind his neck as she rose to a sitting position, her violet eyes all but glittering as she stared at him.

"God, you're just like her."

"Like who?"

"Marie."

He watched her throw her feet over the side of the bed, her back to him. His gaze skimmed the sexy lines of her back and bottom.

"How so?" he asked.

"You're both—I don't know—holier than thou." She glanced over her shoulder. "Whatever happened to everyone deserving a fair trial? To everyone having her day in court?" Her hands twisted into the top sheet. "God, you're so judgmental."

Tommy squinted at her. "Jena, I didn't say anything one way or the other." He rested his hand against her back finding her tighter than she'd been before he'd given her a massage. "If you don't mind my saying so, I think you're the one having trouble with this case. It doesn't matter what Marie or I think. Patsy Glendale is your client. That's where the story begins and ends."

"Yes, well, if you don't mind my saying so, I mind your saying so." She gave a gusty sigh. "I don't know why I said anything anyway. You couldn't possibly understand."

He squinted at her. "Oh? Why? Because I lack the mental capacities?"

She moved out of his reach for something on the floor. "Where in the hell are my slippers?"

Tommy wasn't sure how the conversation had degenerated at such an alarming rate but he did know he didn't like it. Essentially she had just called him a dumb jock. Of course he couldn't understand what she was talking about. He played hockey. And hockey didn't require anything but brute strength, right?

He realized she was waiting for an answer to her question. "I put them in the closet."

"You what?" She stared at him as if he'd admitted to throwing away her favorite lingerie.

He shrugged. "I kept tripping over them every time I got out of bed. That and Caramel seemed to take a liking to them."

She got up and crossed to the closet, throwing open the door with a loud slam. Tommy covered his chuckle at the display of petulance.

"Jesus…" He watched as she snatched her slippers from the closet floor then stood back and took an eyeful of her clothes. Dry cleaner's hangers screeched against the metal bar as she looked through them. "What did you do?"

Tommy shrugged. "I put the stuff you brought home from the dry cleaner away."

She turned to stare at him. "You did more than that! You…you color-coordinated my stuff."

Tommy wasn't entirely sure he liked the way that sounded. "I might have moved a few things around."

"You didn't just move them around…you organized them." She moved a few hangers, then apparently for good measure, set a few hangers askew.

"I...happen...to...like my things messed up." She pointed to where she'd pulled a sleeve of a jacket out and over the clothes next to it. "Do you see that? I purposely did that so in the morning, you know, when I'm still half asleep and in dire need of caffeine, the piece will jump out at me."

Tommy shook his head. "Chaos."

"Maybe. But it's *my* chaos." She slammed the closet door shut. "Leave it alone."

She left the room. Tommy was half surprised she didn't slam the bedroom door after her.

For long moments he lay on the bed staring at the ceiling. Whoa. Now that was a moment he wasn't anxious to repeat anytime soon. Jena was as angry as he'd ever seen her. Of course, it was also the first time he'd seen her angry, so he hoped that was as bad as it got. He scratched his chin and looked toward the empty doorway. The sound of a late-night talk show filtered in to him. He got up and traced her footsteps into the living room. She had crawled up on the black leather sofa and had a wool blanket thrown over her legs. If she noticed him enter, she didn't reveal it. Instead she used the remote to switch through channels like a pro. She'd opened the kitchen door and let Caramel out and now the pup darted around his legs like a furry maniac just released from prison.

Tommy crossed the room and sat down next to Jena. He had on black sweatpants and nothing else.

He interpreted it as a good sign that she didn't move away from him.

"You put up a Christmas tree," she said, her eyes on the television, not on him or the four-foot live tree he'd bought and decorated earlier in the day.

"Yeah. I'd meant it as a surprise." He sank down in the cushions and grinned. "Surprise."

She wasn't amused. Shocker. Considering the conversation they'd had in the bedroom, he supposed that she was of a mind to take issue with anything and everything he'd done.

Of course, the surprise was only part of the package. He'd intended to tell her that he'd finally given in to Kostas's demand that he look up a physical therapist wherever he was. He was pleasantly surprised to find a familiar name in the phone book—an old college buddy. In fact, he'd briefly roomed with Noah Glassman at UCLA in freshman year until he'd moved out with a bunch of fellow players to rent their own house.

If Jena had bothered to check, she would have found a message on her answering machine from him saying he and Noah were going out for a cup of coffee and that he would be late getting in. But, of course, he'd gotten back before she did, which made the issue a nonissue.

"So," she said, finally settling on a channel and looking at him, "what did you do all day? You know, besides reorganize my closets and put up a stupid Christmas tree?''

There was something about the way she said it that raised his hackles, as if she fully expected him to say that he had done nothing.

He itched to tell her that he hadn't done anything.

Instead, he rubbed the back of his neck. He'd learned with his sisters that two wrongs didn't make a right. Obviously she was stressed and needed to vent. And unfortunately he was the closest available target.

''Is there something you'd like to talk about, Jena?'' Tommy knew that was the last thing he should have asked. Insinuating that something other than him really lay at the heart of her black mood would only make matters worse. But he couldn't stop himself.

She opened her mouth to respond, her cheeks smeared with high color.

''Scratch that,'' Tommy said, laying his finger against her lips to staunch the flow of words. ''How about we just call a truce for now?''

Her eyes narrowed as he slowly removed his finger from her mouth and dropped his hand to her bare shoulder.

''A truce? I wasn't aware we were at war.''

Tommy clenched his teeth to keep from responding to that baiting remark. He managed a grin instead, which really wasn't all that difficult to do considering that he'd been looking forward to seeing Jena all day. Then when he'd had his hands on her in the other room and had to force himself to keep his touch platonic no matter how sexual he'd wanted to make it, need swirling low in his belly, it had been all he could do not to turn her over and spread her beautiful thighs to him.

"I missed you today," he said quietly. Truthfully.

She looked at him for a long moment. Then the tension seemed to seep from her, a soft expression settling over her features. "I missed you, too."

He tugged on her arm, pulling her across his lap. He threaded his fingers through her silky black hair and kissed her long and hard, doing what he'd been longing to do ever since she'd stepped in that door.

"Mmm…yes, that's definitely more like it," he murmured, sliding the straps of her chemise down her arms.

She smiled, a decidedly wicked glint in her eyes. "I'm not going to apologize, you know."

He dipped his finger into the front of her chemise and probed her right nipple, bringing it to a tight peak. "Did I ask for one?"

"No, you didn't."

"No matter how much I deserve one."

She tossed back her head and laughed, easing the tension he'd been feeling moments before, transforming it into an entirely different kind of tension he welcomed. He took advantage of the move and nuzzled her throat, drawing his mouth down the long, elegant length of it, then continuing along her shoulder. She shivered.

"Are you cold?" he asked with a raised brow.

Jena wriggled on his lap until she straddled him. "Oh, no. In fact," she said, working her fingers into the front of his sweatpants and stroking the hardening length of him, "I'm starting to get very, very hot."

"Mmm."

Tommy slid down on the couch so that she met him more fully, her softness pressing against his hardness. Now this was definitely more like it. The entire reason he'd come to Albuquerque—to forget about beefs and career questions and lose himself in Jena's sweet flesh. He gazed into her flushed face, liking that the lights were on so he could watch every erotic emotion pass over her features, take in her every movement. Right now she was shimmying out of her panties and tugging on the tie to his sweatpants until his arousal sprang from the soft cotton. She bit her bottom lip.

"In the pocket," he murmured.

She patted both pockets then slid her fingers inside one to take out the condom.

She bit the packet open with her teeth. "I like a man who comes prepared."

He stroked her toned thighs. "With a woman like you, a man always has to be prepared."

Within moments she had him sheathed and was straddling him. He held her aloft, halting her.

"Here, let's get rid of this first." He tugged on the hem of her chemise, then pulled it up and over her head, tousling her marvelous hair. Neither of them cared when the piece of lingerie landed on Caramel, who yelped, then ran for the kitchen, taking the scrap of silk with her.

Incredible. That's what Jena was. From her rose-tipped breasts, narrow waist and dark wedge of hair, she was perfect in every sense. A state that had to come naturally to her, because as far as Tommy could tell she certainly didn't work at keeping her figure. She ate all the wrong foods and took the shortcuts home when walking Caramel.

Jena made a small sound in her throat, demonstrating her frustration by wriggling her hips.

Tommy grinned. "Is there something you want, Miss McCade?"

She grasped his shoulders, giving them a tight squeeze even as she bore down hard against his hands. "Oh, yes, Mr. Brodie. I want *you*. In every sense that it's possible to have you."

"Hmm. Sounds good."

"You have no idea…"

Tommy finally fit her wet heat against him, reveling in her instant shudder.

"Yes," she whispered, her eyes fluttering closed, her spine straightening in anticipation of penetration.

Tommy slowly lifted his hips, entering her mere millimeters, then retreating.

Jena cried out, her fingers grasping him harder.

"Tommy, I..."

She didn't get a chance to get the rest of the sentence out as he pulled her all the way home.

7

JENA RIFFLED THROUGH THE files littering her desk-top. *Where is it, where is it?* There. She fished out the deposition taken the week before from the restau-rant waitress who claimed to overhear Patsy talking about killing her husband. Thumbing through the pages, she found the approximate date the conversa-tion was to have taken place, then compared it to the dates on the copy of Patsy's social calendar that her personal assistant had provided.

Nothing penned in for lunch either that day, or two days prior or after the date.

Jena propped her head on her hand and sighed.

Okay, so maybe the waitress had gotten the day wrong. She looked through the supporting material then made a face. No, she hadn't. There in black and white was a reservation written in for Patsy for the date the waitress had indicated, a reservation made a week prior to the date.

Okay, so Patsy's personal assistant had neglected to make the notation. It happened. People were only human, after all.

But the oversight didn't help Jena at all in trying to contact the friend Patsy had dined with.

Then there was the new evidence piling up. The prosecutor had discovered that Patsy's husband had consulted a lawyer and that everything pointed to his seriously considering asking Patsy for a divorce a month before his untimely demise.

It didn't look good.

But what murder case did?

She reached for her coffee, only to find the disposable cup empty. She tossed it into the garbage can under her desk then glanced at her watch. After six.

Damn. She'd promised Tommy that she'd make it home on time tonight.

Titillating thoughts of great sex and the fear that things were getting serious fast clashed inside her.

She immediately snatched back her hand from where she was automatically reaching for the phone.

"Oh. You're still here, Miss McCade."

Jena glanced up to find the secretary standing in the open doorway. She didn't acknowledge Mona right away, it taking a moment for Jena to move beyond the fact that she had almost called Tommy to apologize for being late. "Yes, I, um, just had a few things I needed to follow up on."

"The Glendale case?"

"Huh?" Jena caught herself picturing Tommy eating alone at her kitchen table and stopped it. Since when had she become an old married woman? "Oh, yes. The Glendale case."

Mona held up a courier envelope. "Then you'll want to add this to the pile. It was just delivered."

"This late?" Jena accepted the envelope, staring at it as if it were Pandora's box and there was no way in hell she was going to open it.

"I thought it odd myself." Mona stood in front of her desk.

"Where's Marie?"

"Left about an hour ago."

Jena put the envelope on her desk. "Figures."

She rummaged around in her drawer for her opener and gained access to the bulging envelope. When she looked up a few moments later, Mona was still standing quietly in front of her desk.

"Is there something more you wanted, Mona?"

The older woman reached up to fuss with her hair. Only then did Jena notice that Mona hadn't pulled it back into her usual bun. In fact, the newly colored strands had been cut and conditioned and were no longer long enough to pull back into a bun. Instead, soft honey-colored curls framed her face, taking at least ten years off her age and softening the angles of her chin and cheekbones. Gone were the large-framed red Sally Jesse Raphael glasses. In their place were stylish black wire rims that any twenty-year-old would feel good about wearing.

Jena sat back in her chair, wondering how she

hadn't noticed the transformation before now. "Wow," she said in awe. "José is better than I thought."

Mona's cheekbones colored slightly. Was that a blush? Jena was pretty sure it was. But because she'd never seen the secretary blush before, she couldn't be entirely sure.

Maybe it was just hot in the office.

"You look…" She gave Mona another once-over. Even though the secretary still wore her staple long dark skirt and white blouse, the ensemble when combined with her hip hairstyle didn't look half bad. "Great."

"Are you sure?" Mona said, unconvinced. "I went in two days ago and…I don't know. I can't seem to get used to the new cut. I keep looking to brush it back."

"No, no," Jena said quickly, "don't do that. Just leave it be. It's incredible." She got up to stand in front of the older woman. She crossed her arms over her chest. "I can't believe I didn't notice."

Mona looked down at her brown practical shoes. "Don't feel bad. No one else noticed either."

Jena lifted her brows. "Not even Barry?"

"Especially not Barry." She cleared her throat, seeming to go out of her way to keep from meeting Jena's eyes. "That's, um, why I wanted to speak to you. You know, if you have a moment."

Jena backed up against her desk. "For something like this, I have all the time in the world."

In the back of her mind loomed an image of sexy Tommy at home waiting for her. She left it right there.

"You see, I was thinking…I mean, I was wondering…if something like this doesn't catch his attention, what else can I do?"

Movement outside the office caught her eye. She watched as Barry left his office, then stood checking the messages at Mona's desk.

"Speak of the devil…"

Mona turned ten shades of red and Jena grinned wider than she had in days.

"Barry? Do you have a sec?"

Mona grabbed her arm. "No…"

But it was too late. Barry was already looking at Jena. After putting the messages back on the desktop he stepped to the office door. "Sure. I always have a second for one of my three favorite girls. Take two if you want. Hi, Mona. Are you still here?"

Mona kept her gaze trained on her shoes. "I was just about to leave."

Jena removed her thumbnail from between her teeth and caught Mona before she could make a bee-line for the door. "Actually, Barry, Mona and I were hoping you'd settle a debate for us."

"A debate?"

Jena grinned. "We need a man's perspective."

Mona looked about ready to slink to the floor and crawl under Jena's desk.

"Okay," Barrie responded.

"You see, she was saying that the man she's dating is making sounds of commitment. And being the modern woman she is, she isn't so sure she's ready for that."

Barry blinked, seeming to look, really look, at Mona for the first time since entering the office.

Jena cleared her throat to punctuate the moment. "I say she should cut and run now, before things get any more complicated," she continued, ignoring the way Barry squinted at his secretary as if sensing something different but not entirely sure what.

Jena cleared her throat again, hoping Barry would take the bait.

Finally he did.

"And what does Mona think?" he asked.

Jena shrugged. "I don't feel fit to repeat it. She'll have to speak for herself."

After a long silence in which Jena suspected Mona was considering how hard she'd have to fling herself at the window to break it so she could fall two floors to the ground below, Barry spoke. "And what do you think, Mona?" he asked the woman who had been his secretary for the past thirty years.

Mona raised her gaze to Jena, revealing the panic on her face.

Oh, God, she's going to flub it, Jena thought, ready to step in.

But before she could, Mona lifted her chin, met Barry's gaze and smiled. "I think I should keep seeing him until he sees the light."

Yeah, Mona! Jena gave a mental cheer.

Then she stared at the woman as hard as Barry was. Was there really a man?

Barry tapped his fingers against his lips. In his mid-sixties, he was still quite a looker with his shock of white hair, distinguished features, and the perpetual tan that made Marie call him George Hamilton on occasion and lecture him on the horrors of skin cancer.

"So?" Jena delicately prodded, feeling suddenly awkward at the silence in the room. She instantly recognized the source of the feeling and nearly gasped aloud. She had that third-wheel sensation that only came about when in the presence of two people enormously attracted to each other.

In fact, if she'd only opened her eyes before now, she would have realized that she felt that way every time she was around the senior partner of the firm and the firm's secretary.

She nearly rubbed her hands together in wicked anticipation. This was going to be fun.

Barry coughed into his hand. "I think Mona should do, um, what she thinks is right," he said and began to turn from them.

Jena not only noticed the way he directed his answer to her instead of Mona, she couldn't help wondering if his response was motivated by jealousy.

"Oh, by the way, Mona," Barry said, pausing at the door, "whatever you've done to your hair? It, um, looks nice."

He left the office.

When Mona finally stopped gaping after him and looked at Jena, she found Jena wearing a huge grin.

"Any more questions?" she asked Mona.

The older woman, still obviously stunned, shook her head. "No. None."

IF JENA WANTED TO THINK of him as nothing more than a brainless jock, far be it for Tommy to prove her wrong.

Tommy made the determination as he sat on her sofa reading the latest sports medicine journal he'd picked up today. Of course, telling Jena he wasn't what she thought wouldn't do the trick anyway. No, that kind of assumption was based on all sorts of deep-rooted misconceptions and prejudices that he thought she wasn't anywhere near ready to admit to. Not just now, but ever. Which made his dilemma all the more difficult.

Oh, yeah. He'd run into his own share of intellectual snobs. Those with degrees who assumed that because he chose to play hockey he didn't have two brain cells to rub together. He rubbed his chin and turned the page to continue the article on the latest in reconstructive tendon surgery. He hadn't known how much it would bother him to find out that Jena was one of those snobs.

Although if he thought about it, she had exhibited all the warning signs. He just hadn't been looking for them. He suspected she chose men she believed her intellectual inferior because, hey, they couldn't exactly pose a threat to her well-maintained life, could they?

Boy oh boy, had she ever chosen the wrong guy for that role.

And boy oh boy, what would she say when he told her he was an M.D. with a specialty in sports medicine? Then again, should he tell her just yet? Doing so might only make her conclude that since he was educated he wasn't truly a jock...and might place their relationship in jeopardy. Whatever that relationship was right now. Beyond mind-bending sex, that is.

He grinned as he rearranged the pile of *Sports Illustrated* and car-collector magazines on the coffee table, then propped his bare feet on top of them. No, let her think what she wanted. He already knew she was in deep with him. How? Well, because he felt himself sliding in deeper with her as each day passed. They'd fallen into a groove. Yes, he still occasionally infringed on the personal space she guarded like a Doberman, but not to the extent he had when he'd rearranged her closet and put up the Christmas tree. He'd learned his lesson. Since then he'd spent his days seeing to rehabilitating his knee…and exploring a possible career change.

Kostas would shit a brick if he knew he was even thinking about quitting the game. The problem was he would end up driving off a cliff if he didn't.

He finished reading the article and caught himself rubbing his knee. The truth was, he was getting a little tired of the battering his body was taking. And as each year passed, the more the injuries piled up, making him a walking barometer for whatever weather system was heading his way. He'd been in Florida when Andrew hit. Two days leading up to it he'd been practically paralyzed with pain and had known the hurricane was going to hit exactly where he was.

Kostas had told him he was insane. No man could predict the weather, especially not with old sports injuries. If that were the case, then all meteorologists would be retired sports heroes.

He cracked his neck. Of course, he was only in the consideration stage at this point. While he'd grown tired of the injuries and watching the severity of them increase as he got older, the truth was that he was at the top of his game. He'd helped win the Stanley Cup for the Aces two years running. Was one of the top-paid players. And he had endorsement contracts coming out the yin-yang. Which explained why Kostas clucked around him like a mother hen on steroids, but he wasn't going to go there. Kostas did what he did because it was his job.

Tommy, on the other hand, had always played hockey because he loved it.

But spending the past two months in a hellish kind of limbo made him take a whole different view of his life. And, yes, while he'd gone to Jena because he knew she would blow every thought out of his head with great sex, he was also coming to see that the step had been the first one he'd taken down a different path. An unfamiliar path that was as exciting as it was daunting, with too many variables and too many forks in the road.

A key sounded in the lock. He briefly looked at his watch as Caramel lifted her head from where it had been cradled in his lap. After ten. He stuffed the medical journal under the sofa cushions and quickly picked up the *Sports Illustrated* swimsuit edition and opened it to the centerfold.

"Hi," Jena said from the hallway.

Tommy grinned. "Hi, yourself." He leaned over and picked up a potato chip from a crumpled bag near his feet. He wasn't sure if Jena would recognize that they were the baked variety and not fried but that was as close he could come to compromising his view on diet for the cause.

"Sorry I'm late," she said, stepping past him and into the bedroom. Caramel jumped off the couch and followed her, nipping at her heels.

Tommy grimaced. Not because he begrudged the dog her feelings for her mistress, but because he found himself wanting to do the same. To nip at those shapely ankles and work his way up those long, lovely legs to the treasure that lay at the apex.

And also because he'd almost said, "You could have called."

Not a good idea. But he was beginning to understand how the many women who had issued the complaint to him over the years had felt. Oh yeah, it sucked to wait for someone and not even be given a phone call out of simple consideration. But just as the whine hadn't made an impact on him back then, he knew it wouldn't affect Jena in the way he'd want, either. No, better to let her think he didn't care what time she popped up. Just so long as she did. Which wasn't too far from the truth.

He cleared his throat and forced himself to stay where he was, listening to the sounds of her stripping out of her clothes and baring all that delectable skin. Drawers opened and closed. Kissy sounds were made as she played with Caramel. Then finally she moved through the hall into the kitchen. Tommy grinned. He'd purposely put her red nightie on top of the others in her drawer earlier. He was happy to see she was wearing it—and without a clue about his minor manipulation.

The refrigerator door opened and closed. The oven

door opened and closed. Murmurs as she talked to Caramel. Then she was striding into the living room.

"There's nothing to eat."

Tommy stifled the chuckle choking him and instead blinked at her. "There's plenty to eat."

Jena's face looked so adorably perplexed that he nearly gave up the ghost right there and then.

Truth was, he'd purposely not made dinner tonight out of simple curiosity. He'd wanted to see what she would do if there wasn't something waiting as it had been for the past week. It wasn't that he felt taken advantage of. Well, okay, there was that too, but it was a lesser consideration. He enjoyed cooking. But Jena's constant complaints about the healthiness of his choices even as she gobbled down his fare did grate on his nerves.

She stared at the magazine in his hands and he grinned and put it down on the coffee table with the other fan magazines. "Actually, I could do with a bite myself. Would you like an omelette?"

Jena made a face. "With that pseudo-egg stuff? I think I'll pass."

He shrugged and got to his feet. "Wouldn't be any problem, you know, since I'll be making one for myself."

He crossed into the kitchen, waiting to see if she'd follow. When he heard her on the phone moments later putting in an order for a pizza, he grimaced. He poured enough egg substitute into a sprayed pan for two then began feeding wheat bread to the toaster. Within eight minutes he filled a large plate with a mushroom-and-cheese omelette, surrounded it with toast lightly covered with margarine, then sat down at the kitchen table, Caramel at his feet.

He wasn't disappointed when Jena took the seat across from him, her arms crossed on the table. "I ordered pizza."

He nodded, pretending an extraordinary interest in the omelette in front of him. He fed a piece to Caramel then forked a piece for himself, piling it on top of the toast before putting it into his mouth. He made a soft sound of appreciation.

"You want some?" he asked after three or four bites.

She made a face. "I think I'll pass." She glanced toward the wall clock. "My pizza should be here soon anyway. I wouldn't want to ruin my appetite, you know."

He shrugged as if it didn't matter one way or the other to him. "I just asked because I don't think I'm going to be able to eat this all myself."

"A shame."

"Yeah. I hate to let good food go to waste."

He waited for her to say he could feed the rest to Caramel, but she didn't. In fact, he suspected she wouldn't because her eyes had avidly followed his every movement since he dug into the light late-night

meal and he could tell she was chomping at the bit
to get a taste. Not that she'd ever admit it.

"I had the day from hell today."

"Did you?"

"You wouldn't believe." Jena scooted closer to the
table. "I mean, I'm no wet-behind-the-ears law
school grad, and I know that the days leading up to
a trial are when you need to be the most diligent, but
today..." She picked up the fork Tommy had placed
on the other side of the plate. "Today I was so busy
putting out fires that I'm not even sure I'm clear on
what started them all."

"The Glendale case?"

Jena sighed. "Yes. Then Marie bailed on me." She
dug her fork into the omelette and talked around a
full mouth. "There was one high point, though."

"Oh?"

He watched her pick up a piece of toast and top it
off with omelette. "Yes." She stared off into the distance as she chewed then swallowed. "You know
about Barry, right? The senior partner who pulled the
three of us into the firm? Well, I don't think I've told
you about Mona Lyndell, the firm secretary, who's
worked for Barry for...well, a lifetime."

Tommy had had his fill of food but was even hungrier now...for Jena.

"Anyway, since coming into the firm nine months
ago, I couldn't help but notice that Mona could give
a good chunk of attention to her appearance. You

know, a good haircut, maybe a change of clothes. Something, anything, to bring her into the new millennium. And I told her so.''

''Did she take your advice?''

Jena sat back and smiled looking pleased, beautiful and knee-bucklingly sexy all at once. ''Yes, she did. And she looks…great. I mean, she hasn't changed her wardrobe, but the change in her hair…well, I didn't really notice it at first. But once I got a good look, I think she looks great.''

Without seeming to realize it, she finished off the remainder of the omelette then put her fork down and wiped her mouth with a napkin Tommy handed to her. ''But I'm not the one who matters. You should have seen Barry's face when he got a good look at her.''

''Barry and Mona?''

''He's a widower, she's an old maid.'' She grimaced. ''Not old, old, but you know what I mean. She's never been married. Doesn't seem to have much of a personal life that anyone knows about…''

She drifted off for a moment sparking curiosity in Tommy as to what she was thinking.

''Anyway, I wouldn't be surprised if the two of them ended up, you know, indulging in some hot and heavy hanky-panky.''

The doorbell rang. Jena looked startled for a moment as Tommy began to clear the table.

''My pizza!''

Tommy watched her get up from the table and rush for the door, Caramel following after her. He watched as she put the pizza on the counter and frowned at it. "Funny, I'm not even hungry anymore."

Tommy chuckled and she made a face at him.

"Very funny." She waggled her finger in his direction. "The way you got me to eat those eggs."

Tommy stepped closer to her. "You know the saying. You can lead the horse to water but you can't make her eat?"

He hauled her to him.

"Are you calling me a horse?" she whispered, slowly moving his hands to her bottom and smiling wickedly at him.

He gave the lush flesh filling his palms a good squeeze. "If you don't start watching what you eat, you might turn into one."

She made a guttural sound, half laughter, half indignation.

He lowered his head and kissed her. "Now what say we go burn off those calories?"

"Good idea. Work up an appetite so I can eat the pizza."

Tommy slid the pizza, box and all, into the refrigerator. "Baby, I don't think you're going to be able to move once I get done with you."

8

THE FOLLOWING DAY JUST before lunch, Jena pulled her cell phone out of her purse and pressed the number for her apartment. She moved out of the way of another attorney trying to get by her in front of the brand-spanking-new district courthouse, then pressed the button to bypass her answering machine message.

"Tommy? It's me. Pick up."

She waited for a few moments as she took in the crystal-clear day around her. One of those rare unseasonably warm days when you wanted to chuck your winter coat and pretend it was spring.

Dead air from the other end of the line. She slowly realized that Tommy wasn't going to pick up and frowned. Maybe he was in the shower. Or walking Caramel. Or grocery shopping. She cleared her throat and left a message. "I thought we could get together for lunch. I only have an hour or so, so give me a call back on my cell when you get this message, okay?" She left the number for her cell then disconnected.

She continued walking away from the courthouse feeling a little awkward. He had a cell phone of his own. She'd seen it on the bedside table. But she realized she didn't have the number to it. There hadn't been a reason to ask for it. He usually picked up when she called her home number. Would he listen to her answering machine messages? They hadn't discussed whether he should one way or the other. She winced, wondering what would happen if another man called and left a message. It hadn't happened so far, but that didn't mean that it wouldn't.

What did Tommy do with his day? He'd been camped out at her place for the past eight days and for all she knew he didn't do anything but read those sports magazines, walk Caramel, and rearrange her kitchen.

She caught herself up short, hating that she sounded so…well, bitchy.

Okay. So he did clean up after himself. And Caramel…well, Tommy appeared to have succeeded where the obedience school and countless attempts on her behalf had failed. She said, ''Sit,'' the dog sat. ''Heel,'' and the dog heeled. It was almost as if someone had stolen her puppy and replaced it with another one that looked just like her, but had an entirely different personality.

And the whole toxic scent issue had magically disappeared.

And what Tommy did in her kitchen not to mention to her person!

Okay, she admitted grudgingly, maybe she hadn't

been able to tell that the things he made didn't have mounds of butter or real eggs or that they were healthy for her. Everything he made was mouth-wateringly good.

She absently smoothed down her jacket lapel. In fact, it appeared he was the wife that she had been wishing for just before she'd opened the door eight days ago to find him standing in the hall looking like pure sin and smelling like pure heaven.

Her steps slowed as she checked her cell phone. Had he really been there for eight days?

The realization provided a moment of pause.

Wow.

And that wasn't the half of it.

She could barely remember a relationship she'd had that lasted as long as Tommy had been at her place. Well, okay, that was boiling it down to dates, equating dates to days. Very few men had made it beyond the eight-date mark, and those, well, had been anomalies, or just good sex when she needed it. And she'd never, ever actually lived with anyone before.

Not that she and Tommy were living together.

She stopped altogether in the middle of the side-walk. Or were they?

Oh, God.

She checked her cell phone again. No response. That left out the shower, which meant that he was out of the apartment.

She punched another number.

"Mona? Hi, it's Jena. Yes. No, everything went great. First time in days, huh? No, I was just calling to ask you to gather everything on the Glendale case together. I'm going to stop by the office and pick it all up and work from home today."

If the secretary found anything unusual in the request, she didn't say anything. Which was good. Because right then Jena didn't know if she was up for questioning. She felt…out of sorts. Downright strange. A man was living at her house and she wasn't sure how that had come to be. Oh, she remembered the great sex. Oh boy, did she remember the great sex. And since he was from out L.A. way, it had been a pretty good guess that he didn't have a place to stay while he was there, especially when he'd basically told her that he'd come solely for her.

But how long would he be staying? Was there a set time? She didn't know how she felt about the prospect of showing up one night to a note that read something like, "Got a game in Syracuse. It was great. Will be in touch."

She drew alongside a park bench and absently sat down. Was that what would happen? Would Tommy simply disappear as quickly as he'd appeared? No warning? No goodbye, it's been swell?

The prospect made her throat tighten.

As did the possibility of his staying indefinitely.

"Oh, boy."

What a mess. She wasn't sure if she wanted him

to stay…or go. And sooner or later he would have to decide on one or the other. They couldn't continue on this way indefinitely.

A mother and her child passed by, the little girl swinging a carved wooden bear dressed as Santa, a Navaho Indian Christmas decoration. Jena blinked several times. Even surrounded by all the trappings since Thanksgiving, she had forgotten that Christmas was a mere three weeks away. Aside from not having very happy memories regarding the holiday, she'd always looked upon it from a single woman's viewpoint. Maybe a few decorations around the house. But never dinner or presents under a tree. She'd bought gifts for Dulcy and Marie months ago and they were tucked away, already wrapped, in her bureau at work.

She stuck her thumbnail between her teeth. Should she get Tommy something? Did she even have a clue about what he would want? An image of sexy black silk boxers and a matching robe crossed her mind and she smiled. But that would be more of a gift for herself.

Her smile vanished. But if she did buy a gift and put it under the tree for him, would that indicate that she wanted him to stay until Christmas? Would the mere suggestion make him run the other way? Would he feel obligated to buy her something? Or did he already have plans to leave?

She flopped back on the bench and sighed. For a woman who had so much going on in her professional life, juggling high-profile cases, starting her own firm with her friends, her personal life was a muddled mess. It wasn't so long ago she'd been able to juggle five men without having to think about it. Now she couldn't seem to handle one.

She banged the back of her head against the bench. Definitely strange. Neurotic. And completely unacceptable.

And something she needed to fix…right away.

WHO KNEW ALBUQUERQUE was a booming sports town? Tommy climbed out of his rental Jeep outside Jena's apartment. Sure, his team, the L.A. Aces, had played an exhibition game with the local WPHL team, the Scorpions, three months ago. That's how he came to meet Jena in the hotel bar. But then there were the pro and semipro baseball and basketball teams, and, of course, the University of New Mexico's active and successful sports program. He'd agreed to meet Noah for lunch earlier in the day and Noah had surprised him with a long, well-thought-out proposal.

He wanted Tommy to come into business with him.

It had taken Tommy a good few minutes to get over his shock, but once he had, he'd listened as Noah explained that while, yes, he handled some patients with sports injuries, general occupational injuries—such as carpal tunnel syndrome and back injuries—

were his specialty and he and his partners could really use a sports guy.

Him. His general thoughts of returning to medicine had now turned into a viable option. He might finally be able to put his medical degree to work.

He shook his head and grinned. Dr. Tommy "Wild Man" Brodie. Now there was an image.

He headed across the street. And why not? A lot of his nonsports-playing classmates had been surprised when he'd picked hockey over medicine. He'd graduated in the top three of his class and completed a brief but comprehensive residency at Minneapolis General Hospital. He'd always been taking some course or another since graduation and had even kept current in the latest diagnoses techniques and treatment so it wasn't like he would be walking around in the dark.

He scratched the back of his neck. Of course, outside his residency he hadn't had hands-on contact with patients. But Noah had assured him that he could hire his own experienced staff and that Noah would even sit in on appointments with him for however long it took for him to get comfortable.

It had entered Tommy's mind that Noah felt sorry for him and was offering him a Twinkie. But Noah had laughed at him and asked if he had any idea what kind of money was in sports medicine nowadays. Given what Tommy and his insurance company and the team plunked down annually on him alone he could imagine it was a handsome sum. So Noah had convinced him that the profit potential was to credit for the invite.

And, of course, it wouldn't hurt the practice to have hockey star Tommy "Wild Man" Brodie working with them either. The PR value alone would be worth bringing him, even if he never saw a single patient.

He slowed his step as he spotted a familiar car. The sleek silver Lexus SUV with CUDA for barracuda spelled out on the license plate was hard to miss. He blinked against the late afternoon light at Jena's apartment windows. What was she doing home during business hours on a Tuesday afternoon?

Jena. Home. Now.

Instantly all thoughts of his conversation with Noah vanished and his libido kicked up. A little afternoon nookie would be just what the doctor ordered.

Compensating for his bum knee, he took the steps leading to the second-floor apartment two at a time and unlocked the door with the key she'd given him. There. There she was, sitting on the sofa in her sweats reading a magazine. He drew closer, intending to jump her sexy little bones right there and then. Until he saw which magazine she was reading. Namely, the ones he kept stashed under the sofa cushions.

Uh-oh.

He grasped the top of the magazine and slid it from her fingers until she was forced to look up at him.

Her smile hit him somewhere between his groin and his solar plexus. Damn, but she had a great smile.

"I was reading that."

He slapped the magazine closed. "Yeah, but were you understanding it? I picked them up at the doctor's office and even I can't make heads or tails out of them. And I've had most of the injuries listed in there."

Well, the first part was true. The particular issue she'd been reading he had picked up at Noah's office. She didn't have to know that the rest of them he'd bought himself.

She laughed quietly as if relieved about something. "I didn't know you were going to a doctor here."

He shrugged and tossed the periodical to the coffee table next to the other magazines. "It was that or Kostas was going to track me down and drag me back to L.A."

"Kostas?"

"My sports agent."

She pulled her knees up to her chest, covering his favorite parts of her. He rounded her and sat down on the sofa next to her.

He stretched his arm across the back of the sofa. "What are you doing home so early? Wait, don't tell me. Your client copped a plea and the case is closed."

She leaned her head against the back of the sofa and looked at him. Really looked at him. "You know, I don't even have the number to your cell phone."

He squinted at her. She was acting...different somehow. More contemplative. "Easily fixed." He fished out a business card from his pocket, picked up a pen from the coffee table where he'd been filling in a crossword puzzle, then scribbled the number to his cell on the back. He handed her the card.

"That's Kostas's info on the front. You can always get a hold of me through him if you need to."

She seemed to consider the information.

"So," he said, snaking his hand over the back of the sofa and fingering the soft strands of her hair. "What are you doing home so early?"

She gestured toward an overstuffed briefcase. "I thought I'd work at home today. You know, one of the benefits of being the boss."

He leaned toward her and kissed her full, luscious lips. She tasted like herb tea. Mint herb tea. Like the kind he'd stocked in the kitchen a couple of days ago. He grinned. "Had I known that, I would have requested you work here over the past week."

She laughed. "And a lot of work I would have gotten done, too."

He tugged at the neck of her sweatshirt as if trying to peer at the treasures under the soft gray cotton. "You mean you plan on getting work done now?"

"Mmm. That was the plan."

"And how..." he took her hand and led it to his growing arousal, "um, firm was that plan?"

She slid down a little on the sofa until she was flush

with him. "Not as firm as other plans, I'm beginning to think."

He nuzzled her neck then followed with a long swipe of his tongue. She giggled and moved closer to him.

"Tommy?"

"Hmm?" he said, busy pushing the hem of her shirt up to reveal the lacy white bra she wore.

"You wouldn't just up and disappear and leave a note behind in your wake, would you?"

What an odd question. He drew back slightly to gaze into her questioning eyes. What had made her ask such a thing? "It depends."

He watched her swallow hard, obviously torn between needing to know the answer to her question, and the heat building between them. "On what?"

"On whether that's what you want me to do."

She flattened her palm against his erection through his jeans and pressed against him. She kissed him languidly. "No. It's definitely not what I want you to do."

"Good. Then I won't."

She gave him a small, sexy smile. "Are you always this amenable?"

"Always."

"I knew there was something I liked about you."

"Like" seemed to be far too tame a word to describe what was passing between them. Although this was virgin ice for Tommy, he sensed he knew the way. Perceived that the feelings expanding in him were powerful, natural and very, very right.

He couldn't seem to drag his gaze from Jena's expressive face. There was something different about her today. Something he couldn't pinpoint, but that drew him irresistibly to her all the same. Her soft, emotion-filled gaze was in contrast to her urgent, provocative touches. The mix caused a chain reaction of sensation in him. His chest grew tight even as his groin heated up.

He got up from the sofa and swept her up into his arms.

She gasped. "What are you doing?" she whispered, grasping his shoulders.

"I'm taking us somewhere where I can do what I have in mind."

She restlessly licked her lips as he headed for the bedroom. He was vaguely aware of Caramel nipping at his heels. He stopped just inside the bedroom, scooted Caramel out then closed the door. "Sorry, girl, but this isn't for public consumption."

Jena laughed throatily as Tommy gazed down at her lying in his arms. The sudden realization of the trust such a hold required hit him in the stomach like a sucker punch. In fact, the trust she'd so generously shown since he arrived at her apartment door made him feel oddly…welcome. She hadn't hesitated to give him a key to the place. She'd gone off to work for the past week leaving what basically amounted to a stranger in her apartment. Yes, while they connected on a physical level, they knew very little about each other beyond the bedroom. Yet the connection they did share...well, it allowed for emotions he couldn't imagine feeling at any other time, any other place.

Seeming to sense the seriousness of his thoughts, Jena stopped smiling and returned his gaze with equal gravity. Had she been considering the same thing? Was that the reason behind her question in the living room?

Had she been wondering when the time would come when he would have to leave?

He laid her sideways across the bed then slowly tugged the sweatpants and panties from her long legs, then her sweatshirt and bra. Her pale skin seemed to glisten against the black bedding, the waning sunlight from the window slanting across her toned stomach.

Tommy's breath hitched in his lungs. She was so damn beautiful. Not just outside, but in. She had more balls than half his male friends, yet could be so utterly feminine, it made him dizzy.

She reached up and tugged his shirt out of his jeans, then hooked her fingers inside the waist of the dark denim, popping the metal buttons one by one with her thumbs while he shrugged out of the shirt. Her eyes shifted and darkened as she looked at him. No matter the state of his knee, he worked hard to keep his body healthy. The superficial physical benefits were of a secondary concern to him, but he was filled with pride when Jena looked at him that way, as if she was hungry and the only item on the menu she wanted was him.

"Come here," she whispered.

What man in his right mind would be able to resist such a sexy invitation? He climbed on top of the mattress, nudging her thighs apart with his good knee while reaching for one of the condoms on the nightstand. She took it from him. Tommy braced himself for her feathery touch, gritting his teeth as she cupped his balls in one hand, fondling them, and rolled the cold rubber down the hot length of him with her other hand, the combination of hot and cold making him even hungrier for her.

Finished, she positioned him against her slick entry. Tommy stared down into her beautiful face as he entered her slowly. She briefly closed her eyes and swallowed, her hands bunching the sheets as she fought to maintain eye contact. Tommy watched a flush creep across her skin, down her neck and over her breasts. He withdrew slightly and slid into her again, very slowly, very deliberately. The fire that ignited along his nerve endings was different, somehow. He supposed it could be the slower pace he was setting, the long, languid strokes of her heat surrounding him. Their lovemaking was usually urgent and greedy and demanding.

Jena arched her back, thrusting her breasts into the air as he slid into her to the hilt. A low moan escaped her parted lips and her eyelids fluttered closed, losing the battle to keep a visual connection. The move freed Tommy to sink into the sensations overpowering him. To give himself completely over to the feel, the smell, the touch of her. She was so, so wet. So, so tight. And so damn responsive he could come just thinking about the way she swayed into him, taking everything he had to offer, and making him feel like it was too much as she shivered from head to toe.

Tommy couldn't remember when he'd enjoyed sex with a woman so much for so long. Every time was different. One time wild and intense, the next time quick and playful with lots of foreplay.

Then there was now. The passion that filled his gut encompassed his entire body in languid heat. Where usually a steam engine roared through his veins, now lava flowed slowly, torturously, moving him toward a phenomenal conclusion that scared him.

"Oh…oh…oh…" Jena moaned, making soft, throaty sounds he hadn't heard her make before. She usually demanded, directed. Now she appeared as consumed by the languid quality of their joining as he was. And the knowledge ripped the air from Tommy's lungs.

Limbs mingled, bodies joined, he inched toward a height he hadn't even imagined existed. His breathing came in ragged gasps though he barely moved. Beneath him, Jena went rigid with her climax, trembling from head to toe as one long moan that seemed to be ripped from the depths of her belly wove around him, beckoning him to follow.

He did, helpless to stop himself. But rather than feeling as if he'd toppled over some sort of precipice and was falling back to earth, he felt as if he'd been launched along with Jena straight into the air, twirling and twisting and flying. He found it impossible to breathe as he wondered at the exquisiteness of the place they'd uncovered together. His heart beat slow yet hard, pumping blood through his limbs, but just enough. And his climax seemed to go on for so long that he began to wonder if he'd ever make it back.

But he did, although somehow he didn't feel like he was the same man who had been launched into that ultrasensual never-never land. He was completely drained as if he and Jena had been having sex for hours. He lay carefully against Jena, giving himself over to the languorous sensation that swept over him as powerfully as his climax. Jena lazily curved her leg around one of his, rhythmically rubbing.

And when Tommy kissed Jena, he felt as if he was offering up his very heart to her…and that she was not only accepting it but offering her own up in return.

9

"SO WHERE EXACTLY HAVE you been hiding yourself lately, Jena?" Dulcy asked over lunch at Georgio's in downtown Albuquerque, within walking distance of their office. Jena found it ironic that it was the same place where the waitress had allegedly overheard Patsy making her damning comments about killing her husband.

She pulled her gaze away from a waitress across the room, then pretended an intense interest in forking her spinach salad. Spinach salad. Was she really eating weeds? Okay, not weeds, but they were green. Not normally something seen on her plate. "What do you mean? You see me nearly every day at the office."

Marie picked bacon bits out of her own salad and put them on her napkin with her fork. "Personally, I'm convinced she's kidnapped a really hot guy and has him holed up at her apartment."

Jena choked, spinach flying from her mouth and landing in the middle of the white tablecloth. Her friends stared at her.

"I knew I shouldn't have ordered this stuff," she

muttered. She waved for the waiter. "Could you please bring me the filet mignon and take this away, please?"

"Jena?" Dulcy said when the waiter had discreetly cleaned the spinach from the middle of the table, taken her plate and disappeared.

"Hmm?"

"Oh my God, that's it, isn't it? You do have somebody tied up at your place." Marie's blue eyes danced with excitement. "Oh, oh, oh, don't tell me. It's that hockey player, isn't it?"

This time Dulcy choked, but she managed to keep her food inside her mouth. "Hockey player?"

Damn. Jena had thought she'd done a good job of glossing over Tommy's identity when Marie had asked about him after Judge Bullock's Christmas party. Obviously she hadn't done a good enough job because sometime between then and now she had added A to B and come up with a very damaging C.

"You don't mean…one of *those* hockey players?" Dulcy said after taking a long drink from her water glass. "From the night of my bachelorette party?"

Marie cleared her throat. "Uh-huh. You know, the ones with the tight buns…and the really big sticks."

Jena nearly choked again, then generously buttered a roll and stuffed a good portion into her mouth to muffle her words. "Marie doesn't know what she's talking about."

"Uh-huh," Marie said again with a smile.

Dulcy's unblinking attention remained on Jena's face. "I thought you guys closed the club down after I called it a night."

"You didn't call it a night. You snuck off with Quinn, remember?"

"I did not sneak off with him. I…ran into him on my way back to my room."

Jena lifted a finger. "Yes. And ran into him in the elevator. Where you proceeded to have hot and steamy and very public sex."

Dulcy flushed all the way back to her blond roots. "God, why did I know I'd live to regret telling you guys about that?"

Marie snickered. "Yes, well, Jena ran into her hockey player as we were leaving the club. I'd always had the feeling she left her room to go meet him after we said good-night, but I never knew for sure. Until now."

"You don't know anything."

Dulcy cracked a smile as the conversation moved away from her and back to Jena.

"What?" Jena asked, irritated.

The waiter brought her new plate and she made a ceremony out of cutting her meat.

"Oh, nothing. It's just that you have to be one of the single worst liars I've ever come across."

Marie pointed her fork in Jena's direction. "I think it's because you usually tell the truth. Very bluntly, I might add."

''And I think you've both lost the last of your marbles.''

''Uh-huh.'' Dulcy remained unconvinced. ''Anyway, forget all that. How's Caramel doing?''

''Fine. Caramel's doing just fine,'' she said, finding her meat very good indeed. ''Tommy's been—''

''Aha!'' Marie cried, gaining them the attention of nearby diners.

Jena groaned and felt like dropping her head onto her plate. She *was* an awful liar. The worst. The most despicable. What kind of attorney was she, then, if she couldn't bluff her way through a lunch with her best friends without them knowing she was having the best sex she'd ever had in her life with a man who'd essentially been living with her for the past ten days?

Dulcy made a strangled sound. Jena looked up to find her friend trying to suppress a laugh.

''Oh, yeah, little miss innocent over there who slept with the best man a week before her wedding, go ahead and laugh. Keep it up and I promise to make a date to tell that mini-him or her you give birth to in six months all about his or her mother's scandalous escapades.''

''Her.''

Jena and Marie stared at her.

''I mean, it's a she.'' Dulcy's smile couldn't have been bigger without splitting her face in two. ''I found out this morning during an ultrasound.''

"Oh, Dulcy, that's great!" Marie leaned over to hug her.

"Yes, I'm pretty pleased with the information. Quinn is more man than I can handle. I couldn't imagine having another little man just like him in the house."

Jena hugged her friend tightly. Up until now the baby had been an undefined entity, more abstract than reality. But now that they knew it was a girl...the reality of the situation hit Jena unexpectedly full in the heart.

"Does Quinn know yet?" she asked, reluctantly releasing Dulcy.

She shook her head. "No. Seeing as it is a girl I, um, wanted to tell you two first."

Jena felt a suspicious burning sensation behind her eyes.

"Oh, that's so sweet," Marie said.

Dulcy quietly cleared her throat. "And since I have you both alone, I'd like to ask if you both would consider becoming the baby's...her godmothers."

All three of them completely forgot their meals and hockey sticks as they animatedly discussed names and clothing and baby furniture and middle of the night feedings. Jena had never given much thought to children before. They'd always been something somebody else had had to worry about. Not her. Not her close circle of friends. But with Dulcy's pregnancy came the introduction of the topic into her own life.

Dulcy was the first to admit that she hadn't planned to get pregnant so quickly. She'd wanted to enjoy some prolonged time with her new husband first.

Marie…well, Marie wanted a dozen kids. It was the husband part she was having a problem with. Not that she was looking, but she was dead set against her Italian family having a say in who she married.

Eventually, they all began eating again, giving Jena a little too much opportunity for thought. Did she want children? If she had asked herself the question even a month ago, she would have answered with an unqualified no. She liked her life the way it was, thank you very much. Then Dulcy had given her the puppy, something else she'd sworn she would never, ever own. And she'd discovered that she liked having the little fur ball around the house. Liked coming home and opening the kitchen door to find the little stinker unconditionally happy to see her.

Then there was Tommy…

She nearly choked again, this time on her meat.

Dulcy clucked her tongue. ''Looks like you're having all kinds of trouble with your food today.''

''Oh, would you please just shut up?'' Jena said, holding up her hand.

''So…'' Dulcy said, finishing with her meal, ''when, exactly, were you planning to tell us about Tommy?''

Jena shrugged, giving up on her own meal. She

wasn't very hungry anyway. "When there is something to tell."

"So is he staying with you then?" Marie wanted to know.

Jena stared at her.

"What? It's a valid question. He was with that visiting hockey team three months ago, right? From L.A.? And since I don't recall seeing any return visits on the schedule…"

"Since when have you become an expert on sports events?"

"Since I grew up with three older brothers." Marie cupped her glass of iced tea in her hands. "And you're avoiding the question."

Jena stuck her tongue out at her and all three of them laughed.

"Okay, okay. Yes, his name is Tommy. Tommy Brodie. And, yes, he plays for the L.A. Aces."

Her friends remained silent.

She heaved a long sigh. "And, yes, he's staying at my place. Okay?"

"I knew it!" Marie said. "The force of the spinach coming out of your mouth was a dead giveaway."

Dulcy laughed. "She does have a point. The look on your face when she asked if you had a man holed away at your apartment was priceless." Dulcy tucked a strand of her loose blond hair behind her ear. "This must be pretty serious, huh?"

Jena shrugged. "He's just visiting."

Silence fell over the table.

"So," Marie said, "what are we doing for Christmas this year?"

"Christmas?"

Dulcy laughed. "Yeah, you know, the reason all the trees are decorated and you hear carols piped all over the sound systems."

"I know what Christmas is. And I know that it's only a little over two weeks away."

Dulcy pretended to wipe sweat from her brow. "Whew. At least we haven't completely lost you."

"Har har." Jena bit briefly on her bottom lip. "I don't know if I'll be, um, free for Christmas."

Dulcy and Marie looked at each other and raised their brows.

"Oh, stop it already," Jena told them. "The truth is...well, I don't know what the truth is." She grinned. "All I can say is that the sex is...the sex is...wow."

Dulcy cocked a brow. "Wow? This from the woman who tries to share every intimate detail? The one we have to gag to keep from telling us the size, shape and physical characteristics?"

"I'm not that bad."

"Oh yes, you are," Dulcy and Marie said in stereo.

"Okay, okay. Maybe I usually am. But this...this is different somehow, you know?"

Dulcy put her napkin on her plate. "Then you must bring him to Christmas dinner at the ranch."

"Yes," Marie said. "I'll even risk my mother's wrath by skipping dinner with the family to come out to see this Tommy up close and personal."

Jena bit briefly on her bottom lip. "I don't know if he'll be here for Christmas."

"But didn't you just say..." Dulcy let her words drop off.

"Hell, Dulcy, I don't even know if he'll be there when I get home." She sighed as she tossed her own napkin to the table. "God, I hate this feeling."

"Oh my God," Dulcy whispered. "Can it be that our commitment-phobic friend has been—dare I say it?"

Marie leaned forward. "Bitten by the love bug?"

Jena's eyes opened so wide the overhead lights hurt. "What? Jesus, Marie, I haven't heard that term since we were teenagers." She pushed her chair back from the table. "And I am not in love."

Neither of her friends said anything.

The silence was like a pin to her defensiveness. "At least I don't think I am."

Marie eyed Jena as she opened a breath mint and popped it into her mouth.

Jena groaned. "How would I know if I am?"

Dulcy reached over and took her hand. "Trust me, sweetie, you're demonstrating all the signs."

"Oh, great. That's all I need. To fall in love with the big lug."

The only problem is she was afraid Dulcy was

right. She already had fallen. Deep. And she didn't have a clue what to do about it.

"WHAT, ARE YOU ON CRACK?"

Tommy sat back in the kitchen chair and moved his cell phone from one ear to the other. Kostas was in prime form today with the drug reference. Not that he could blame his sports agent for his reaction. He didn't think many people in his life would react positively to the words he'd just said to Kostas.

"Nope," he sighed. "I've never had a clearer thought in my life."

He tossed a doggie treat to Caramel who was doing her best at playing dead. Not bad. Except for the panting. She rolled upright to slobber up her treat.

"Damn it, I knew this trip was going to spell trouble," Kostas said after an extra long pause. "A doctor? You want to become a friggin' doctor? Where's the respect in that, I ask?"

"What you really mean is where's your eighteen percent, isn't it?" Tommy chuckled and scratched Caramel's ears, earning him a sloppy hand bath.

Kostas cursed a blue streak. "Yeah, and then there's that. You know what your little career change is going to cost me, Brodie?"

"I don't know. A lot?"

"You're damn right it is."

Tommy heard the rustling of papers on the other end of the line.

"Look, the doc says I can't play on my knee for the rest of this season at least, anyway. And that's when my contract is up for renewal."

"You've played with worse injuries."

"Maybe I have. But not anymore."

Silence reigned on the other end of the line, then Kostas astutely asked, "Don't tell me. This doc with the prognosis is the old friend you were talking about? The one who wants you to join his practice?"

"You won't find a doctor that will tell you anything different, Kostas."

"Try me."

Tommy's humor slipped. Yes, he'd expected Kostas to be upset, but when everything was said and done, he'd hoped that he and the high-strung Greek were friends above and beyond all else, including business. They'd vacationed together in the Greek islands. Played countless rounds of golf. And had even double-dated. Hell, he'd even taken the guy home to Minnesota for family visits.

"Are you going to make this difficult for me, K?" Tommy asked.

Silence.

As he waited for Kostas to respond to his question, he watched Caramel turn and tap toward her water bowl where she made a mess out of getting a drink.

Finally, an exasperated sigh.

"You're killing me here, you know that, don't you, Brodie?"

Tommy grinned, relieved to hear that Kostas had made the choice he'd hoped he would. "Yeah, I know."

The squeak of a chair being turned. "Have you told anyone else of your decision yet?"

"Nope. I thought you should be the first."

An image of Jena flashed through his mind and he questioned his decision not to tell her about his medical past or his possible future in sports medicine. He ran his hand through his hair and puffed out his cheeks. That was going to be an interesting conversation. *"Oh, Jena, by the way, I earned my medical degree while playing college hockey and I'm trading in my hockey stick for a tongue depressor. Just thought I should let you know."*

"Don't tell anyone."

Tommy squinted. "Kostas, I'm not going to change my mind, if that's what you're hoping."

"I know you won't. That's what sucks about this whole thing."

Tommy chuckled.

"No, what I'm looking at is the bigger picture. If you announce your planned retirement now..." Tommy cringed at the word. Made him sound and feel old. "...Then all those endorsement contracts I have lined up will dry up like that." Tommy heard the snapping of fingers. "Wait until the end of the season and you—and I—can move on with our pockets nicely lined."

Tommy felt he owed his friend that much. And,

hey, a little extra cash couldn't hurt either. His mother volunteered at a homeless shelter and was always complaining about there not being enough services for young mothers there. The money might be enough to let her open her own home for homeless mothers and their children.

"Done," he agreed.

"That's my boy!"

It had been a long time since anyone had called him a boy and it made him puff out his chest a little.

"So now are you going to tell me where you are?"

"Somewhere between New York and L.A."

A long line of foreign curse words filtered through the phone. Greek, Tommy knew, although he didn't understand a single one of the words, which was probably just as well.

"Fine. Fine. Don't tell me where you are then."

"I won't."

"At least tell me where I can send your Christmas present."

"Aw, you bought me a present?"

"No, but I will if you give me an address."

"Nice try, K."

"Okay, okay. How about a date when you'll be back so I know when to schedule the photo and commercial shoots?"

"I can go from here. I'm wide open. If that changes, I'll let you know."

"Good, good."

"Only make it after the holidays, okay?"

A brief pause. "Who is she?"

Tommy rubbed his forehead. Kostas knew him too well. "Who is who?"

"The woman you're spending the holidays with, that's who."

"Nobody you know," he said, wondering if he would be spending the holidays with Jena. He hoped he would. But they somehow never got around to discussing the present, much less addressing the future.

A few minutes later he finally wrapped up the conversation and thumbed the disconnect button. Talking to Kostas was always a trial in patience, but given the nature of this discussion, it ranked right up there with the most draining.

He rubbed his face and thought about taking a shower. What remained was how and when to tell Jena what he had in mind.

The thought alone made his throat tighten.

How would she react to the news? He honestly couldn't say. He wasn't sure if it was because she was anything but predictable. Or given the gravity of the news, his mind threw up a mental block every time he thought about it. Likely a little of both.

But he didn't think he should show his cards just yet, not until she did a little hand-showing of her own. It still rankled to think that she believed him little more than a mindless jock capable only of performing well on the ice—and between the sheets. And while

holding up his medical degree would give him some
personal satisfaction, it wouldn't eradicate the original
problem. Nor would it help determine her real feelings for him.

Sure, while he'd witnessed some true, raw emotions from her, he couldn't be certain how deep they
went. They could be merely sex-related, or of a short-
term nature. All he knew was that he had to find out.
On his terms. In his way.

And regardless of the outcome, he wouldn't give
up. Because if there was one thing *he* was certain of,
it was that what he felt for her he would feel forever.
It was very much like what he felt for his parents, his
sisters, his friends all rolled up in one, with the added
dimension of overpowering lust.

He was *in love* with Jena. And he *loved* her. He
cared how her day had gone, if something bothered
her. He was worried for her safety and her health, as
well as wanted to touch her in a way no other man
had before.

But springing a marriage proposal on her wasn't
going to work. She wasn't a traditional girl given to
traditional conventions. She was a collage of different
elements he didn't think he'd ever be able to pin
down or figure out. But he was coming to accept that
that was okay. It was enough to know how he felt.
No matter what she did, he would love her. Together
or apart.

Only he planned for it to be together.

Caramel plopped her furry butt down on the floor at his feet. He stared at her.

"So what are my odds, short stuff? Do you think I have a chance in hell of getting her to admit she loves me?"

Caramel lifted onto her hind legs so she could rest her paws on his knees, then dropped her face on top of them. Her puppy dog eyes wide and wet, she then gave a long sigh.

Tommy chuckled and gave her an affectionate pat. "Well, I guess that's one way of putting it." He got up and led the way to the bathroom. "Come on, what's say we go smell good for Mama."

10

JENA WAS EXHAUSTED. After lunch with Dulcy and Marie, she'd squeezed in some power-shopping time. Sure, she'd already long since bought for her friends, but, well, there was Mona to think about now. And she hadn't considered buying something for Dulcy's yummy husband, Quinn. Then there was Barry Lomax.

Okay, so she really hadn't gone shopping with them in mind. She'd used them as an excuse to shop for a certain yummy guy of her own. The other gifts…well, aside from being an excuse, she wouldn't look too desperate if she had other presents under the tree. And with the additions of Dulcy and Marie's gifts, Tommy would have to do some searching to find his presents as she fully intended to put them in the back and under the rest of them. She didn't want him to feel pressured into buying her something. After all, she had no idea as to his financial health. If he wasn't playing, he wasn't getting paid, was he? And all his money could be tied into assets not easily liquidated, like homes and cars and the like. She didn't want to make him uncomfortable if he couldn't afford to buy something for her.

Not that she wanted anything...

God, was that really her thinking this way? Jena paused on the steps to her apartment, the wrapped packages weighing down the two bags she held. She closed her eyes tightly. She felt like an unqualified emotional mess. Questioning, then requestioning herself, then doubting yet again. This wasn't the person she looked at in the mirror every morning. The woman who had spent the past thirty years molding herself into one of the best criminal defense attorneys Albuquerque had to offer. Given her background, she subscribed to the philosophy that childhood was something you survived—adulthood and being in control of your own destiny being the reward. She'd come a long way since she lost her parents at ten. She'd grown up, gone to and graduated from college, attended law school, then landed her first legal position. And, damn it, she relished being the one in charge.

Funny, then, that she sensed that control shifting. Her focus slightly askew.

Slightly? Hell, she was downright out of whack, period. All since one hunky jock appeared on her doorstep and turned her world upside down.

And she was deathly afraid that Dulcy was right. She was in love.

What was she going to do?

Scratching sounded from the other side of her apartment door, snapping her from her reverie. She climbed the remaining few steps then unlocked the door, bracing herself for Caramel's attack.

"Did you miss me? Did you?" she asked the rambunctious puppy. Caramel did a little dance, her furry rump swaying wildly as she barked.

"An entire day's worth of training out the window in one blink," Tommy said from where he stood leaning against the doorjamb to the kitchen. He grinned.

Jena's mouth watered as she looked at the man who occupied so much of her thoughts lately. She petted Caramel for a few more moments then lifted to her feet and picked up the bags again.

This wasn't healthy, was it? The strange swelling of her heart? The acceleration of her heartbeat every time she spotted Tommy? She remembered thinking that the guy should come with some sort of warning label. The problem was that she didn't think she was in any mindset to read it just then.

Dressed in a dark pair of cargo pants and a tight-fitting black shirt, he looked as good as the smell of whatever he was cooking in the other room. And one hundred percent like a hard-body jock.

"Hi," she said, feeling awfully awkward in her own apartment.

"Hi, yourself." He indicated the bags. "You need any help with those?"

"No!" she said too quickly.

He cocked a brow and she made a face. So much for being subtle. "I'm just going to get changed and, you know, put this stuff away."

"Ten minutes, then?"

"Ten minutes?"

"Ten until dinner."

"Oh. Yes. Sure."

Jena scrambled for her bedroom where she immediately closed the door then leaned up against it, her heart beating a scary tattoo in her chest. She heard Caramel on the other side of the door and quickly opened it and closed it again until she was staring at the quizzical pup.

"What?" she asked.

Caramel cocked her boxy head at her and made a small sound.

Jena pointed a finger at her. "Don't give me any guff, dog, or else you go back out."

Kicking off her shoes, she bypassed the nosy mutt and headed for her closet. She hung up her blouse, then the remainder of her suit, then scrounged around for something decent to wear. Something better than the sweats and robes she had taken to donning lately. She chose a cream-colored pair of jeans and a soft suede blouse and held them up to look in the mirror. Too...light. She wanted to look casual, but not too casual.

She pulled out a plum-colored pair of cords and a matching shirt. Too...eggplant.

Finally she settled on pair of red jeans and a clingy black top. She reached to pick up the discarded garments to find Caramel sitting on top of them, avidly watching the display. She shooed her away and hung the clothes back up. Then she crossed to the bed to sit down and put on her shoes only to throw herself across the mattress lengthwise. She plucked her pillow from under the covers and bunched it up under her face. Burying her nose in the soft mass, she took a deep breath. Pillows were highly underrated, in her book. It was with her face burrowed into a pillow that she did her best thinking.

And, oh boy, did she have some thinking to do now.

Caramel jumped on the bed next to her. She moved to shove her off, only found herself patting her instead. The pup settled in next to her, curving into her side with a soft sigh. Jena smiled.

''Maybe dogs are underrated as well, huh, Caramel?''

A soft whine, then the pup rested her head on her outstretched paws and blinked at her.

Jena closed her own eyes and took another deep sniff of her pillow, detecting Tommy's unique scent on the soft pillowcase. What was she going to do about Tommy? More importantly, what was she going to do about her feelings for Tommy beyond continue to have the most amazing sex with him? Yes, while the love bug might have bitten her hard, she didn't think she was in the market for anything long-term. Even if Tommy were interested, which she highly doubted he was. Come on, he was used to being on the road, traveling from town to town, venue to venue. She doubted he stayed in one place any longer than a few days, maybe a couple of weeks, at a time. Before long he'd surely grow tired of Albuquerque and would be on his way.

The problem was that this wasn't about him. It was about her. If, in fact, Tommy's leaving was in the future, she needed to decide what to do about that. Did she wave him off and tell him to come back for a visit any time he was available? Did she tell him it was nice but that was it?

Or did she ask him to stay?

Jena's chest tightened to the point of pain. Well, it was an option, wasn't it? Asking him to stay?

But we don't have anything in common, she argued with herself.

Even though she recognized the argument as a shield against fear, she also saw that it was true. She and Tommy did, it appeared, have very little in common. Her career included keen mental strategy and concentrated attention. His depended on a great body and physical activity. He wouldn't even wear a tux, for God's sake, when everyone else had one on. And she'd bet gallery openings and charity events were definitely not his thing, while both were included in her favorite pastimes. And while she'd stuck close to home recently, it was usually rare for her to see the inside of her apartment. Aside from her caseload, she liked to play as hard as she worked, and that included going out a lot. Tommy, on the other hand, appeared happy to commandeer her sofa and palm the TV remote.

But when it came to sex...well, they were both definitely on the same page.

She turned her head in the other direction while she absently stroked Caramel.

What to do?

She yawned, her muscles remarkably languid. She'd better get up before she fell asleep. She didn't have time for a nap right now. She needed to figure out what she was going to do about her life and the man in the other room.

That was her last thought before she took one last sniff of her pillow, then drifted off to sleep.

TOMMY RAPPED SOFTLY on the bedroom door. He hadn't heard any sounds coming from inside for at least twenty minutes. No response to his knock. He absently rubbed the back of his neck. If she were doing something in there that she didn't want him to know about, he didn't want to barge in.

"Jena?"

Nothing.

Grasping the door handle, he cracked it open...and found Jena fast asleep across the bed.

Tommy opened the door the rest of the way and stepped quietly inside. He gazed down at the dog peering at him groggily, then at Jena's face. God, she was beautiful. Even knowing that her impromptu nap threw a monkey wrench into his dinner plans, he felt like he could stand there and stare at her forever.

He picked up a throw off a nearby chair and carefully laid it over her. She didn't budge, not even when he brushed her silky black hair from her cheek. Dinner could wait. And so could he. No matter how much he wanted to crawl on top of that bed with her and spoon. Simply because he knew that spooning would lead to much, much more. And he and she needed to have a long-overdue talk.

He turned to go and nearly tripped over the bags she'd brought in with her. He grimaced. Was there anything in there that needed to be refrigerated? He bent over and peered inside then snapped back upright. Christmas presents? Giving her a quick glance, he picked up a small package wrapped in red on the top. ''For Tommy'' was written on the small gold card.

Despite himself, he grinned. She'd bought him a Christmas present.

And if she found out that he'd been snooping, she'd probably have a fit.

He carefully returned the package to the bag then backtracked out to the hall, leaving Jena and Caramel right where they were…and wondering what the gift-buying expedition meant.

He quietly closed the door and stood for long moments with his hand on the knob. More importantly, he wondered if Jena had considered what it meant.

He frowned and headed back toward the kitchen to try to salvage dinner for later.

SOMETHING WET TOUCHED Jena's face. She blinked a couple of times, seeing the outline of something light and furry, but it took a few moments to register that Caramel was licking her cheek.

"Eeeeuw."

Jena shot up on the bed and pushed her tousled hair from her eyes. She stared at the pup who interpreted her quick movement as playtime and started tearing around the bed like a dog gone insane.

"Just how long were you doing that?" she asked the dog. She breathed against her hand and sniffed. "It's okay for you to have doggie breath, but revolting for me to have it."

A sharp bark made Jena jump as she squinted at the clock. It was after ten.

Oh, God!

She leapt off the bed and rushed first one way then the other, her head feeling like it was stuffed with pillow stuffing. Caramel followed, nipping at the hem of her pant legs.

Tommy…

And dinner. She'd missed dinner. The low rumbling of her stomach served to further emphasize the point.

She glanced toward the closed door, wondering why Tommy hadn't woken her. She checked her shopping bags. Safe. She quickly stashed them in the closet. After seeing to some repair work in the mirror, she opened the door and was nearly knocked over by Caramel who stampeded her way toward her papers in the kitchen. Jena peeked into the room in question to find it dark and minus one particularly attractive hockey player.

The sound of a sports announcer came from the direction of the living room. Slipping out of the bedroom and closing the door after herself, she made a brief pit stop in the bathroom, then went to stand in the archway leading to the living room.

There on her black leather couch, in all his jock glory, reclined one thoroughly delectable Tommy "Wild Man" Brodie. His bare feet rested on the pile of magazines he'd accumulated since he'd arrived— his legs were crossed, as were his arms...over his broad, mouth-wateringly toned bare stomach.

"Um, hi," she said, stepping farther into the room.

Tommy held up a finger. "Hold on. It's the last ninety seconds of the game and...yes!"

He shot to a standing position and cheered so loudly that Jena jumped. Her gaze darted to the television screen where a seemingly ten-foot wide player completely camouflaged in a football uniform had just scored a touchdown.

Jena looked back to Tommy, thinking that she wouldn't mind scoring herself.

That was, of course, if she could gain the attention of the guy who had first invaded her apartment and her life such a short time ago.

Tommy sat back down and patted the spot next to him. "Come here."

He still hadn't looked at her and Jena wasn't all that sure how she felt about that.

But she did take the seat next to him.

A minute and twenty seconds to go in the game. How bad could that be?

Unfortunately she found out that it could be very bad indeed. A minute and a half was stretched out to fifteen minutes. Fifteen minutes in which she longed to sneak into the kitchen and get something to satisfy her growling stomach. Or touch the guy next to her who was so totally engrossed in the game she wondered if she existed to him at all.

She made a face. Okay... "I'm going to the kitchen."

She started to get up when Tommy stayed her with a hand. "No...wait. You've got to stay to see this one last play."

Jena stared at the screen, trying to decipher the appeal of watching mud-caked men run around in someone's large backyard trying to knock each other over while one of them ran with a ball made out of pigskin. She failed miserably. She sighed as the television zoomed in on a huddle. Okay, so they had great butts. But a woman could only take so much looking at them and not being able to touch.

Speaking of touching…

She slowly turned her attention to the man next to her.

"Tommy?"

No response. He appeared completely oblivious to her presence.

"Tommy?"

"Hmm?" he finally said although he didn't budge an inch.

Jena curled her legs underneath her and scooted in closer to him. "I was just thinking…"

Tommy moved over, away from her, a couple of inches. "Thinking what? Oh, no! Did you see that?"

Jena smiled as she flattened her hand against his gloriously bare abdomen. Okay, so she could kind of see where having your man distracted could be a blessing. She bent and pressed a kiss to the hot flesh then swirled her tongue along it.

Tommy appeared not to notice.

Okay…bolder measures were called for.

She slid her fingers down toward the waist of his pants and tunneled them inside the thick material, instantly finding his arousal and cupping it.

A quick intake of breath, but still his attention was on the game.

One button…two buttons…then Jena was staring at the one-eyed bandit who had also been forgotten about because of a stupid football game.

"Jena?" Tommy asked quietly. "What are you…? Oh."

She fastened her mouth over the thick, pulsing length of flesh and took as much of him in as she could. If his whoosh of breath was anything to go by, she'd finally gained his full attention.

She blinked up to find him watching her through hooded eyes, the loud cheers after some play or another on the television completely forgotten.

Jena swirled her tongue around the thick shaft then added suction, loving the taste of him, the feel of him, against her tongue. Tommy's eyes closed and his hips bucked involuntarily off the couch.

Oh, the power. The complete sense of having someone at your mercy. Of knowing that you could provide such mind-stealing pleasure that they instantly forgot about their surroundings. Gone was the football game. A mere shadowy memory was her hunger for food. Part of the past were the drastic mood swings she'd experienced all day.

Jena curved her fingers down the base of his arousal and into the hair beyond, then squeezed the soft orbs just beneath. A primal growl ripped from Tommy's throat as he threaded his fingers through her hair and urged her down even farther. She took in as much of his length as she could then slid back up, then down again until she felt him stiffen beneath her, on the verge of orgasm.

Jena slowly removed her mouth, then sat up next to him, leaving his member exposed and vulnerable, thrusting up in the air as it was without a single person to give it the attention it craved. A glance toward the television told her the game had ended.

Tommy groaned and cracked his eyes open to stare at her.

"I haven't had anything to eat since lunch," she said, making a move to get up. "Do you want anything?"

"Way wrong question," he said, his voice gravelly and full of threat as he caught her around the waist.

Jena blinked at him innocently.

"Get over here and finish what you so wickedly started."

She made a ceremony out of brushing the area around her mouth. "But I did finish."

"Uh-uh." He shook his head, a dark grin spreading across his striking face. "You were just getting started."

She tried to get up again and he almost roughly held her down. "Tommy. I'm hungry."

"Funny. Suddenly so am I."

He pounced on top of her, making quick work out of stripping her of her pants. Before she knew what was happening, he was between her legs, lapping at her in a way that set all her limbs on fire. So unexpected was the move that she was instantly rendered little more than a sack of lust. Around and around her sensitive skin his tongue roamed, then he fastened his mouth around the tight bud and gave a generous suck.

Jena gasped as she dug her fingernails into his bare shoulders. "Oh, yes... There. Mmm."

The flames flicked over her entire body and the weightless sensation in the pit of her belly spiraled outward and outward until...

Tommy pulled away.

Jena stared at him openmouthed and fuming where he peered at her between the V of her knees.

"You know, I think I am a little hungry, after all. I'm going to fix myself a sandwich. You want one?"

Tommy took in the heated flush of Jena's magnificent skin and the way she lay bonelessly against the black leather like she was incapable of even the tiniest movement. Ah, yes, two could very definitely play at the teasing game. And if he wasn't wrong, he'd just trumped her ace.

If a brainless jock is what she wanted, then a brainlessjock was what she was going to get.

Honestly, he hadn't been giving much attention to the football game. At least not until she came into the room. He'd been aware of the moment she'd stirred in the bedroom and decided now would be the perfect opportunity to hone her view of him as a brainless jock.

Only not even he could have anticipated her mind-blowing response. At least not until she pulled away and left him hanging.

He started to get up from the couch, glad that he'd been able to give her a bit of payback. Only he wasn't prepared for her launching herself at him, pinning his back to the couch, and straddling him like a she-devil set on a very decadent mission.

She reached up and stripped herself of her shirt and bra until she was completely nude, her breasts jiggling as she moved, her nipples hard and pert. She pointed a finger at him. "You and me? We need to have words."

He grinned and grasped her hips as she sought and found a condom in the side pocket of his cargo pants. "Words aren't exactly on my agenda right now."

"After," she said, rolling the condom over his pulsating flesh, then settling herself over him.

Tommy groaned as she sank all the way down, taking him into her slick, tight flesh in one smooth glide.

He gripped her hips to hold her still, only she batted his hands away, then sought leverage by pressing her palms against his shoulders. His gaze glued to her swaying breasts, he watched her pump him for all she was worth. Up and down, up and down, accepting his flesh then sliding from it, the friction of flesh in flesh chasing every thought from his mind except the magnificent woman having the ride of her life.

Flames licked and roared, quickening his heartbeat, accelerating his pulse, as Jena worked her magic.

Oh, yeah. This he could definitely get used to....

11

"DATE NIGHT," THE NOTE READ. "I'll pick you up at six."

Jena read the note she'd found on Tommy's pillow that morning, then stuffed it back into the pocket of her skirt. After a night of decidedly naughty sex, she was surprised to wake to find him gone and the note in his place. In fact, his obvious absence was what had chased her from bed when she'd been seriously considering calling in another sick day.

She glanced around her office, then nudged her watch around to look at the face. Only one in the afternoon. Could time move any slower? She was going insane wondering what he had in mind for the night. He didn't indicate casual or dressy. But given his hate of tuxedos she could safely assume that a night at the opera wasn't in the offing.

Of course, the last thing she should be thinking that moment was of anything outside the office. The Glendale case was getting even more complicated by the minute.

She fingered the fax in front of her from Jo Logan, a local private investigator who the firm had on re-

tainer. Miss Lorena Taylor, age twenty-four, was
Glendale's mistress for the past two years. Attached
was a picture of a pretty brunette bent over what
looked like books. Jena squinted closer at the photo.
Law books. She turned back to the first page. Enrolled
in the University of New Mexico's School of Law.

Oh, great.

Jena propped her head on her hand and sighed. Did
the prosecutor know of Miss Taylor's existence?
She'd chance a guess and say yes. She pulled the file
with the D.A.'s discovery information on it. No information listed on Lorena Taylor. Not surprising. But
if her P.I. had picked up on it, it was a pretty safe bet
that the prosecutor's office had the information as
well.

Just another straw on the pile weighing down Patsy
Glendale's case.

She leafed through the other files on her desk, looking for the background check on the victim, Harrison
Glendale. She couldn't recall there being mention of
a mistress in the initial report. Where was it? She
went through her file cabinet, then got up and stepped
toward the lobby and Mona's desk.

Funny…Mona was always around somewhere. In
fact, the woman had the downright uncanny ability of
knowing when you needed something and popping up
at that moment holding just what you wanted.

But not now.

Jena glanced at her watch again. Too late for lunch.

Anyway, Mona usually took hers at her desk. And the busy state of the desk itself indicated that she hadn't left for a dental appointment or taken the afternoon off. She fished a message Mona had taken for her out of a small pile and frowned. The private investigator had called, probably to verify that she'd gotten the last bit of damaging information.

"Mona?" She stepped toward Marie's office. The redhead was on the phone with her back to Jena talking about tort law. No Mona. Dulcy's office was dark since she was working at home. She stopped in front of Barry's open office door. He wasn't in there but, like Mona's desk, it was obvious he was around somewhere.

Jena blew out a long breath. Figures. The only time she actually went looking for the woman and she was nowhere to be found.

She headed toward the rest room. Might as well see to that before going back to her desk.

She pushed open the unisex bathroom door and froze in her tracks. There against the sink was exactly who she'd been looking for…with Barry Lomax. And she hadn't interrupted an innocent kissing session either. Barry had Mona's long skirt hiked up to her thighs and his hands were clearly doing something not even Jena could see.

Thank God.

Mona gasped, Barry chuckled and Jena crossed her arms over her chest and grinned.

"I wondered where the two of you were."

Barry stepped back and Mona was flushed so deeply red she fairly glowed.

"Mona, do you know where the Harrison Glendale background file is? I've been looking all over for it."

Mona reached behind her and collected something from the counter at the same time as she tried to straighten her skirt.

"Oh, thanks," Jena said, accepting the file.

She opened the door. "As you were, you two."

Barry cleared his throat. "I trust this information stays in this room?"

Jena blinked at him. "What information?"

Barry smiled at her. "Good girl."

Jena let the door close after herself then leaned against the wall next to it with a satisfied smile.

MISERABLE. UNQUESTIONABLY, irreversibly and utterly miserable. That's what Jena looked like. And Tommy couldn't help but be amused by her.

Okay, so maybe he could have told her what he had in mind and suggested she dress accordingly. But he suspected she would have dressed inappropriately anyway. Let's face it, while Jena liked jocks, she probably hadn't attended a sporting event in her life. And the Stingley Coliseum where the New Mexico Scorpions were playing...well, it wasn't the most hospitable place in the world. And if he'd been dressed in a curve-fitting dress and high heels and a

coat that was never designed to keep anyone warm…
well, he'd probably be looking pretty miserable himself right about now.

He turned his head to try to erase any signs of
amusement just in case Jena took it into her mind to
whack him in the head with one of the shoes in question.

"People actually like coming to these things?" she
muttered, pulling his jacket a little tighter around her.

Tommy indicated the crowd. "Why do you think
they're here?"

He watched her eye the enthusiastic audience, but
it didn't change her unhappy expression one iota. "I
thought only family members and friends of the players actually came to these things." She eyed a few
attractive young females near the protective glass.
"And women on the make?" She looked at him, her
gaze questioning.

Tommy raised his brows. "What?"

"Hockey players have groupies?"

He grinned. "You're surprised?"

She nodded. "I'm surprised. Looks like too much
work to me." She tugged on the coat again. "And
too damn cold."

"Funny, I thought the party you took me to the
other night was colder."

"No comparison."

"To you, maybe. To me…" He shrugged.

She managed to look even more miserable if that were possible.

"What are you thinking?"

"What?" she asked.

"Just now. What were you thinking?"

She shook her head. "About how long it's going to take me to warm up when we finally leave this place."

He eyed the snug skirt of her dress. Damn, but she looked good. Every guy in the place attached or otherwise, had noticed her the instant they walked into the rink. "Do you want to go now?"

She looked at him hopefully. "Do you?"

"Nope. There's another period to go yet."

She made a face.

"But we'll go if you want to."

"No. You went to the party. It's only fair that I suffer through this."

Tommy sat for long moments pretending interest in the game between the New Mexico Scorpions and the Odessa Jackalopes. The clean sound of the skates gliding against the ice. The clack of sticks battling for the puck. Then the puck itself smacking against the retaining wall after an unsuccessful goal attempt. Ah, this was his element. But strangely enough he was satisfied just sitting in the stands with Jena. He didn't feel the need to get out there and play himself. A new sensation for him because he'd never been able to just sit and watch a game before without burning to get out on the ice.

Of course, having Jena next to him was largely to credit for that.

He scooted closer to her on the hard wood bench, brushing his leg against hers. Denim against black stockings. ''Here,'' he said, sliding his arm under the edge of the coat and drawing her closer. She instantly snuggled against his side. ''Better?''

''Marginally.''

He chuckled then dropped his hand to her bottom, well hidden by the bulky black satin stadium jacket he'd draped over her shoulders when they first got there. ''How about now?''

Her eyes flashed as she looked up at him. ''A little better.''

''Only a little.''

''Mmm-hmm.''

He tugged on the front of the jacket then moved his hand so that his fingers were cradled between her toned thighs.

She made a soft sound in her throat. ''Now we're talking.''

There was some action on the ice and the crowd let out a roar and got to their feet. Tommy looked to see the home team had just made a shot on goal and had recovered the puck for another shot. He removed his hand from Jena's warm thighs and stood up himself to see over the heads of the people in front of them. The next attempt was successful, ricocheting off the goalie's skate and arching out the back of the net.

He cheered along with everyone else.

A moment later he realized that Jena hadn't joined him. Instead she was glowering on the bench where he'd abandoned her.

"Tommy!"

He heard his name being called from somewhere behind him. He looked up to see Noah Glassman some ten benches behind them. Jena's frown deepened.

"I thought that was you," Noah said, coming down to greet him. "But I wasn't sure until you called out, 'Just shoot the sucker.'" Tommy vigorously shook his friend's hand and shared a laugh. "I didn't know you were going to be here tonight."

Tommy wasn't about to tell Noah that he hadn't known this was where he was going to end up either. Not with Jena listening in no matter how much she pretended noninterest in the exchange.

"Noah I'd like you to meet the reason I'm in Albuquerque." He didn't miss the rising of Noah's brows. No, he hadn't shared why he was in town and Noah hadn't asked. "Jena McCade, this is an old school buddy of mine, Noah Glassman."

Jena shook hands with Noah and exchanged a few pleasantries, and all in all tried not to look completely miserable.

"So you're the reason he's here," Noah said good-naturedly. "Well, I hope my partners and I will help give him some more reason to stay."

JENA INSTANTLY FORGOT about her aching feet, the bone-chilling cold and her overall disappointment in Tommy's choice for a date as she smiled at Noah. "Oh?" she said calmly. "Do you have an interest in a hockey team?"

"Oh, Lord no," Noah laughed, nodding toward whomever he had left in the stands behind them. But not before Jena caught the brief glance between him and Tommy. While she couldn't see Tommy's face, she had seen Noah nod slightly. "If you'll excuse me, I'd better be getting back to my son. It was nice to meet you, Miss McCade."

"Jena, please."

Noah grinned, said a couple words to Tommy about a meeting in the morning, then he headed back up the middle stairway.

Tommy turned and indicated she sit back down. Jena did, readjusting the jacket, although no longer needing it for warmth.

"He seems nice enough," she said.

"Mmm." Tommy's attention seemed overly intent on the game although nothing seemed to be happening at the moment.

"Where did you say you'd met?"

"Noah and I? Oh, at college."

"And you've kept in touch over the years?"

Tommy gazed at her, his eyes full of humor. "Not much really."

"And where did you two run into each other again?"

Tommy's humor spread to his generous mouth. He feigned the need to loosen his collar. "Why do I suddenly feel like I'm on the witness stand?" He narrowed his eyes as he took her hand and sandwiched it between both of his. "You did say you're a defense attorney and not a prosecutor, didn't you?"

"Yes, but that doesn't mean I don't come across the odd reluctant witness or two. Then, of course, there are those prosecuting witnesses that need a bit of debunking."

"And which would I be?"

"Pardon me?"

"The questions. Which witness would I be?"

Jena twisted her lips. She could tell by his expression that she wasn't going to get any further than she had already. Which wasn't that far at all. "Neither. You're my date."

He straightened the jacket on her shoulders. "And not a very good one at that. You're not having very much fun, are you?"

"Oh, I don't know," she said, sighing against him. "I think things just got a little more interesting."

Crowd noise rose again and Tommy leapt to his feet, shouting at the players on the ice below. Jena rolled her eyes to stare at the rafters and hoped she wouldn't turn into a human Popsicle before it was time to leave…

IF EVER HE'D NEEDED A reminder that the clock was ticking on a decision about the direction of his and Jena's relationship, running into Noah at the ice rink had been it.

Tommy avidly watched Jena crack into a particularly stubborn Alaskan crab leg, then attack the meat inside the shell with gusto. He caught himself grinning. When he'd chosen the place, he'd fully expected her to be as miserable there as she'd been at the ice arena. At least before he'd introduced her to Noah…

She tilted her head, her violet eyes full of wicked pleasure as she sucked on the shell to get the last of the meat. Oh, yeah, Miss Jena McCade very definitely looked like a woman with a bone clenched between her teeth. And he had the feeling that she wasn't going to let it go until he gave up the ghost.

He took a healthy swig of beer. In fact, he'd be sorely disappointed if she did give up. While the night hadn't gone completely the way he had planned, it didn't hurt to have Jena think there might be more to him than met the eye.

''So,'' Jena said, liberating a napkin from a pile and wiping her hands. ''Noah looks like a nice guy. How did you two meet in college?''

''Dorm mates.''

"You roomed together?"

He nodded as he stuck a forkful of food into his mouth.

"When?"

"In college."

"I meant, which year?"

"First."

"You mean to tell me you weren't bunking with all the other athletes?"

He grinned. "By the end of the year I was. I shared a house with them."

"But you and Noah became close enough that you remembered each other from then?"

He cocked a brow. "Yes, as a matter of fact, we did. He was in several of my classes and we always got on well."

"Which classes?"

Tommy gave a mock look around the seafood restaurant, his ridiculous plastic bib crinkling as he did. "I could have sworn I heard a judge's gavel."

Jena laughed softly, drawing his attention to her decadent mouth. "Sorry. It's just that…I don't know. You've said so little about yourself since you've been here and tonight seemed a good opportunity to make up for lost time."

"The same applies to you."

She shifted in her seat and sat straighter, pondering his comment as closely as she'd considered her food.

"Go ahead," she said, clearing her throat. "Ask anything you want."

Tommy considered her. There was one question that had bothered him ever since she'd casually mentioned it a few days ago. Or at least that's what she'd have him believe. "How did your parents die?"

Tommy watched every last drop of color drain from Jena's face, and the amusement vanish from her eyes.

"I'm sorry," he said and meant it. "I didn't realize it was such a sore subject."

Jena shook her head after taking a long sip of her diet soda. "There's no way you could have known it was sore." She shifted again but this time the movement was closer to a fidget. "And it's a reasonable question. I'd told you my parents had died. It's only natural that you might wonder how they died."

"And when."

She quietly cleared her throat again, her eyes on the food in front of her, though he doubted she saw it.

"And when," she said so quietly he nearly didn't hear it.

For long minutes she continued eating in almost slow motion. But Tommy's mind was on everything but the food in front of him. He knew the same applied to her, but he suspected she needed the crutch, the space to gather her thoughts. And he gave it to her.

Even without her saying a word, Tommy sensed the magnitude of what she was about to say. Knew that what she would share meant the world to her and had changed one little girl's life forever.

And that that little girl was the beautiful, wounded woman now sitting across from him.

"I was ten," she said, the words seemingly ripped from her chest, although she had said them softly. "I don't know—I suppose up until that point I had a normal childhood. An only child, as we, um, already established."

Tommy smiled faintly at her feeble attempt at humor.

"Not a family in the sense that Marie understands family. Or even Dulcy. But my parents and I...we were *our* family. A family of considerable means that lived an idyllic life in the upper crust of Albuquerque society. I always thought of it as *The Valley of the Dolls*...without the sex and the drugs, of course." She quietly cleared her throat. "Back then I only knew the title of the book, not all the irony it included."

Tommy nodded and discreetly held up his hand when the waitress started to approach the table. She took the hint and steered a path clear of their table.

He was surprised, and touched, that Jena was saying what she was and he didn't want to chance her clamming up again, although he suspected that by this point she had tuned everything out. That the world beyond the intimate spotlight he had placed on their table didn't exist. There was no one to judge her. No one to blame her. No one to pity or shame her. Only him. And all he wanted to do was care.

"Marie and Dulcy and I all lived within a few blocks of each other, although sometimes it seemed a world away, and we used to play together, but they couldn't have lived more different lives. But not, um, only because of what happened to my parents…"

She fidgeted as if incapable of facing the truth herself. Tommy moved to ask her not to go on. He couldn't stand to see her so uncomfortable.

Only he sensed she needed to feel the pain…and needed him to feel it with her.

She sat up straighter and met his eyes. "You see one night after a particularly nasty argument, my mother hit my father in the back of the head with a champagne magnum."

The words seemed to fall into some dark void that existed in the middle of the table between them. They'd been said quickly, in a no-nonsense, matter-of-fact way because, Tommy guessed, saying them any other way wouldn't have been as honest.

"Dom, of course," Jena finally added, her smile a bit tight. "She, my mom, couldn't have known the bottle had hit him, my father, just right. Had no way of knowing that a movement she'd seen in dozens of movies could have resulted in something so serious.

Couldn't have known that in one split second she had killed her husband…and my father.''

Her voice wavered. Tommy reached out to take her hand. He was relieved when she allowed him to take it. Her skin was damp and as cold as ice.

She sniffed loudly, appearing to have passed over the rough part. Or at least to have been infused with some sort of strength. Perhaps relieved that he hadn't reacted in a negative way to the incongruity of the situation. ''An accident. That's what it was. And I knew it was. I was there, watching from the stairwell. I saw my mother try to wake my father. Witnessed her crumpling into nothing as she cradled his head in her lap, blood all over her new white dress.''

Tommy had never had someone lay herself so completely bare to him. Never had someone trusted him so implicitly. He tried to imagine the ten-year-old Jena all laughter and light changing into a different girl the night her father died. And he felt the insane urge to go back and make it all right again for her.

''An accident. Only back then, there really were no accidents, were there? At least not in our neighborhood. Had my father accidentally killed my mother…'' She seemed to catch herself and swallowed hard. ''Well, they probably wouldn't have arrested him, much less have charged him with her murder. But Mom…''

Her words drifted off and she stared at some indefinite point over his shoulder.

"She…she came home early the next morning. The housekeeper had agreed to stay the night with me and I was still in bed. I'll always remember that day. The way she looked still wearing that white dress stained with my father's blood. The heartbreak in her blue eyes. I thought…I thought she was back for good. That the police had realized their mistake and that she and I would get through this together. It wasn't until after I heard the gunshot five minutes after she left my room that I realized that she had been saying goodbye to me."

Tommy didn't know what to say. Didn't even know if she expected him to say anything. Jena had just shared one of the most horrific stories possible with him…and it had been her life. He felt angry…betrayed…and so damn protective of the woman across from him that he wanted to gather her up in his arms and never let another person hurt her again.

Himself included.

"Come on," he said, grasping her hand and getting to his feet. "Let's get out of here."

He draped her coat over her shoulders, shrugged into his own, then peeled off a couple of large bills and left them on the table. Moments later, he was pulling Jena from the restaurant, not stopping until they were near where he had parked his rental car. Only he couldn't wait until they got there. Around them the quaint street in Old Town was decorated with lit paper bags Jena had told him were called *farolitos* as they'd walked to the restaurant. Around them other couples strolled and families headed to dinner. But all Tommy could see was Jena.

He pulled to a stop next to a small adobe building that sold Cochiti pottery Christmas sets and gathered Jena into his arms, shielding her from passersby and squeezing her so hard he was afraid she couldn't breathe. But he couldn't help himself, damn it. The pain that had been hers was his now, too. And he wanted to shield them both from it.

With the very tips of his fingers he brushed her hair back from her face again and again, her skin extraordinarily pale under the unforgiving street-lamps, her violet eyes moist and filled with raw emotion.

"I hate what happened to you," he whispered harshly, eyeing every inch of her face.

She merely looked at him, her thick, dark lashes spiky from tears.

He closed his eyes and rested his chin on top of her head. "And, damn it, Jena, I love you so damn much I hurt."

12

JENA FELT EXPOSED IN A way she never had before. Her relationship with Dulcy and Marie had developed over a period of years. It was only natural that she felt okay talking to them about things she wouldn't dare bring up in mixed company. Their friendship was something that she hadn't chosen, hadn't sought out, it had always just been there.

But with Tommy…

Outside of her friends, no one else knew the entire story of her parents' deaths. Oh, sure, rumors were batted around in so-called polite society from time to time. Especially when she'd come into the money that had been put in a trust for her when she was twenty-five and a new law school grad. She'd decided to reenter the life she had once known as her own, although at first she'd been a little hesitant, worried about what her parents' old friends said about her. Then very quickly she'd accepted that the past would always be a part of her shadow and she'd learned to work with it. And while a great deal of her ballsy behavior was born of necessity, she admitted to getting a charge out of shocking some of the most unshakable pillars of society.

Then in a few short days Tommy had come in and demolished all that. He'd skillfully stripped away the layers she'd carefully covered herself with and left her exposed, raw and aching.

And telling her that he loved her had scared her to death.

"Are you okay?" Tommy asked later that night as he lay next to her in bed.

She smiled at him in the dark. "I thought you were asleep."

"I thought the same of you until you just made that funny sound."

"I don't make funny sounds."

"Yes, you do. It sounded like something startled you."

She absently finger-combed the unruly cowlick back from his forehead and watched in fascination as it flopped back down again. "You should know by now that nothing startles me."

Tommy propped his head on his hand. "I know that's what you'd like me to think. What you'd like everyone to think."

She heard herself make the sound this time and was doubly shocked.

"See," Tommy said, taking her hand and kissing the back of it.

Jena settled down more comfortably against the

sheets. "What I see is that you're an arrogant know-it-all jock who doesn't know when to stop."

She rubbed her head against his bare chest then sighed.

"Tommy?"

"Hmm?"

"Do you ever think about kids?"

Silence, then, "Kids?"

"Yes, you know, children."

"As in general? Or as in having them?"

"Having them." The sheets rustled as she turned to face him. "Do you want to have a mini-you running around calling you Dad? Or ten mini-yous? Or have you pretty much decided that children are out of the picture, you know, given that you spend so much time out on the road and all."

"I won't be doing that forever, Jena."

"And you avoided my question."

He grinned and pulled her closer to him. "Yes, I did. Now go to sleep. It's too late for such an important discussion."

Jena knew he was right. While she'd been wide-awake mere minutes before, now she felt incredibly groggy. She snuggled closer, absorbing Tommy's warmth and allowing herself to drift off to sleep.

"THE JURY SPECIALIST HAS arrived," Mona said from the doorway of Jena's office. "Would you like me to show her to the conference room?"

Jena moved the phone receiver from her left to her right ear. "Sure. If I'm not off the phone in five minutes, remind me that she's waiting, okay?" Then she waved Mona away.

Mona turned to leave and Jena turned back to her files, trying to find the one with the private investigator's information while she waited to be put through to her. The P.I.'s secretary had wanted to take a message but Jena had requested to wait, so she had no one to blame but herself. Truthfully, she was afraid that if she didn't talk to the P.I. now, she would forget under the avalanche of other stuff she had yet to do.

Marie popped her head around the doorway. "Three interns signed on and are busy at work strictly on the Glendale case."

Jena exhaled deeply. "Thanks, Marie. What would I do without you?"

Marie came fully into the office. "Oh, I don't know. Dump Glendale as a client, maybe?"

Jena stared at her friend. "I really don't need to hear this now, you know?" She found what she was looking for and slipped the papers out from a pile of others. She slapped it down in front of her. "Besides, I thought we resolved that issue."

Marie grimaced. "Yeah, so did I. But for some reason I just can't get it out of my head that this is a case of pure, one-hundred-percent premeditated murder."

Jena threw up her free hand. "Well, that does it

then, doesn't it? I should just close the case and tell Patsy to get another attorney. Four days before trial. Then you and I should retire from law and start our own psychic network.''

''Oh, we're in rare form today, aren't we?''

Jena thought of the three days that had passed since the night when she and Tommy had shared more than just crab legs. She'd probably seen him a whole forty-five minutes combined. Forty minutes of that had been wild sex, the other five the getting out of and back into clothing.

This morning when she'd tried to apologize for being so busy, he'd said he understood. But she'd left the apartment wondering if he truly did. Despite the closeness they'd shared the other night, now she didn't think she could feel farther away from him. Or maybe because of the closeness she noticed the distance. Either way, she was afraid she was losing him. What really sucked was that she was never really sure she'd had him in the first place.

''Jena?''

''Ms. McCade.''

Marie and the voice on the receiver spoke at the same time, adding to the jumbled mess that currently constituted her life. She told the P.I.'s secretary to hold the line, then asked Marie to look in on the jury specialist she'd flown in from Boston. She was the best in the business, not to mention the most expensive, and Patsy was going to need the best if she hoped to escape life in prison. Or lethal injection. Although New Mexico hadn't executed anyone since 1976, capital punishment was still an option.

"Thanks for holding," she said to the private investigator's secretary, giving Marie a thank-you smile as she left the office. She stared down at the report on Miss Lorena Taylor and her alleged ties to Harrison Glendale. Nowhere was there a contact number or address for the law school student.

"No problem," the secretary said. "I just wanted to tell you that Jo just left. She said she'll catch up with you out on the road, sooner if she misses her plane."

Jena sighed. Figures. "Okay. Should you talk to her before I do, tell her it's urgent I speak to her."

"I will."

Jena slowly hung up the phone and tried to figure out how in the world she was going to spin this one if she didn't hear back from the P.I. before next week.

TOMMY SAT AT THE KITCHEN table, alone, for the fourth time in as many nights. Even Caramel seemed to sense the change in the atmosphere around the apartment. The neighbor was back to walking the dog during the day while Tommy juggled physical therapy sessions with meetings with Noah and his partners to further cement their plans. At night, Tommy was convinced that Jena's continued absence was due as much to her running away from him as her dedication to her client.

''Looks like we're on our own again tonight, short stuff,'' he said quietly.

Caramel thumped her tail where she sat in front of him.

Tommy glanced at his watch. He knew better than to start cooking anything that had to be eaten now, especially since the grueling period just before trial had begun. But strangely that didn't seem to stop him from hoping that Jena would pop up anyway, take a brief half hour off work and come home to see him and eat dinner.

She didn't even call.

Tommy clapped his hands, as much to jar himself out of the malaise he'd fallen into as to wake up Caramel. ''Hey, girl, what's say you and I go for a walk?''

Caramel instantly got up and went for her leash in the other room. Tommy grinned and followed. Evening walks recently had consisted of squatting next to the fire hydrant in front of the building because Tommy had been afraid of missing Jena.

''That's a girl,'' he said, patting Caramel affectionately, then attaching the lead. He grabbed a coat and headed out, knowing the action was little more than another attempt to face what was really troubling him.

He dry-washed his face then opened the door out onto the brisk December evening. Caramel led the way out and paused near the hydrant in case that was as far as they were going. Tommy turned right instead, earning him a happy yap and a couple gorounds with the leash as Caramel circled him.

He chuckled. "Have I been that bad?"

Caramel barked again, then commenced sniffing everything in sight in case another canine had beat her down the path.

What was really troubling him? that little voice in the back of his mind whispered.

He wanted to tell that squeaky wheel to shut the fuck up. But he'd done so so often over the past couple of days it now emerged as a child's whiney mantra. "The end is near... The end is near..." played over and over again in his mind until it nearly drove him crazy.

He supposed a guy had a tendency to think that way when he told the woman he was dating that he loved her...and she made no comment whatsoever.

Tommy moved his right leg around a bit, testing the knee even as Caramel led him on relentlessly as if afraid if she hesitated he'd head them back home. His knee was feeling better. This morning he'd even considered heading to the local rink and giving it a trial run. Noah had told him that he could start considering it, and he had been thinking about it for some time even before Noah's input, but knew he wasn't anywhere near playing status yet. Of course, both of them knew he never intended to play another game again. The only one reluctant to accept that fact was Kostas.

But even he'd been better recently. He'd stopped hounding Tommy about his decision and instead focused on ways to work around it, intent, as he put it, "on milking the cash cow for all she was worth before putting her down for good."

It didn't bother Tommy that he was the cow. He'd long since grown used to being considered a piece of meat, a commodity whose price depended on how well he performed.

But one place where he refused to be treated like a piece of meat was with Jena.

He'd finally decided to tell her about his medical background and the career path he was considering...no, had decided on. But had yet to catch a chance to share the news. Either she was too busy, or she'd say something to distract him. And what she'd said about her parents had definitely distracted him.

Finally convinced that he wouldn't call a halt to the walk if she stopped, Caramel hesitated near a tree, sniffing around and around the base, giving Tommy a break from the quick pace she'd set.

The moment Jena had shared her past, he didn't think he'd ever felt closer to another person in his entire life, his family included. And for that one night he'd felt a peace, a completion, he'd never known. The sense of tranquility had been lost the next day though, when she didn't come back to the apartment until after midnight, and even then barely dared to meet his gaze. He knew that instead of allowing herself to surrender to the emotional intimacy that had begun developing between them, she was using it as an excuse to close him off. And now with this big case and her being gone all the time, Tommy didn't know how to breach the gap that was widening between them.

Then again, there was always the possibility that he'd been fooling himself. That the only one who had felt the closeness was him.

Caramel succeeded in wrapping her leash around the tree while Tommy was otherwise occupied and stood swaying her furry butt at him.

He sighed. ''I guess you're not the one to ask for advice about my life, huh? You can't even sniff a tree without getting into trouble.''

Caramel barked and Tommy grabbed her collar in one hand and released the leash with the other. As he untangled the lead, he wondered if his life was as complicated as he thought. Or if his emotional investment was making it seem so.

Not that it made a difference. While some might be able to separate emotion from action, he was finding out he wasn't one of them. And he was recognizing that fact on a multitude of fronts. From his career as a hockey player to his choice of home bases, emotion was playing a significant role in every decision he made.

He only hoped he didn't live to regret his decision to shake things up a bit with Jena. But if things didn't change in the stalemate that was currently their relationship, he was afraid some drastic measures might be called for. And one of them was definitely leaving her.

THIS WAS IT. THE LAST night before the trial officially began. The jury had been seated. All the prep work had been done. And Marie, Dulcy, Mona and Barry had all kicked her out of the office promptly at five to get home and get a good night's sleep.

Only sleep was the last thing on Jena's mind. She thumbed through her opening statement, her gaze drawn yet again to the man stretched out on the couch next to her. His gaze was glued to the television set across the room. A football game was on, but the sound was off, the captions crawling across the bottom of the screen. Caramel was lying on the couch next to him, her head across his jean-clad legs.

Oh, how she wished she were that dog right now.

She turned her attention back to her statement.

Tommy moved. "You want something to drink?"

"An apple martini would really hit the spot right now," she said without looking up.

"Will an orange juice do?"

Jena grimaced. "No soda?"

"I'll see if I can scare one up for you."

She finally looked up, finding a thoughtful expression on his handsome face. "Thanks," she said quietly.

She tried to concentrate on the papers on her lap but failed when she realized Tommy hadn't moved from where he stood next to the sofa, Caramel by his side.

She finally looked up. "What is it?"

He stared at her for a long moment, then shook his head. "Nothing."

He finally left the room, taking Jena's peace of mind with him.

Not that she really had any to begin with, but what little control over her thoughts she'd had vanished at his peculiar behavior. She glanced at the TV to find he had switched it off.

That was odd…

She craned her neck to see that the light wasn't on in the kitchen, but it was on in the bedroom. Odd seemed to be the name of the game lately where Tommy was concerned. During jury selection, he had been quiet when she'd returned to the apartment. In fact, they hadn't even had sex for the past three days.

Jena's eyes widened. No sex?

Okay, so she'd been exhausted when she'd come home late all three nights, but that hadn't affected Tommy's abilities to woo her into at least a hot quickie. One touch of his capable hands on her back, massaging her muscles, and she was putty, his for the molding.

Putting her statement, notepad and pen on the coffee table, she got up and stepped toward the bedroom. She hadn't made any sounds to tip Tommy off to her presence, but her gasp definitely gained his attention. He rose from where he was stuffing his things into his duffel bag. Covering his chest was a University of New Mexico sweatshirt.

"What are you doing?" she whispered, grabbing hold of the doorjamb for fear that she might fall over otherwise.

Tommy ran a hand through his sexy dark hair. "Something I should have done about a week ago."

"I…I don't understand."

He shook his head, then sat down on the bed. "That's why I didn't do it a week ago."

Jena crossed to the other side of the bed and sat down so that they were back to back. She felt like someone had dropped a bag of ice down the front of her sweater. The shock of it deemed her capable of doing little more than staring at the wall. She was vaguely aware of Caramel coming to stand in the doorway, but couldn't sum up the energy to address the confused canine—essentially because she was just as confused.

"Look, Jena, the last thing I want to do is hurt you." Tommy's quiet voice came from across the bed. "And I certainly hadn't planned on doing this the night before your big trial, but—"

"Screw the trial."

She felt his weight shift on the bed.

Jena held her ground, refusing to look at him.

"You know, I could have taken the coward's way out and left you that note you talked about."

She glanced down at her shoes. "You mean the one where you thank me for the good time, tell me you'll call, then disappear from my life?"

"That would be the one."

"Is this really any better?"

She felt his hand on her shoulder, instantly filling her with conflicting emotions. One part of her wanted to shrug him away; another, stronger, traitorous part longed to lean into the touch, if only to revel in it for as long as she could.

"This doesn't have to be the last time we see each other, Jena."

"Oh?" She was disappointed to find that tears clogged her throat. She fought to keep her voice even. "You mean the next time you find yourself in town? Or with another injury? You don't think I'm just going to let you in the next time you show up on my doorstep, do you?"

"No."

Her heart dropped to the floor next to her feet. He wasn't coming back. The mere thought made her feel sick to her stomach.

He shifted again and she felt the heat of his body mere inches behind her. His other hand grasped her other shoulder. His fingers tracing small circles in her muscles were meant to relax, but instead increased the riotous emotions crowding her chest.

"What I mean is that I won't show up uninvited again." He brushed his nose against the back of her hair, causing her to shiver. "From here on in, you have to ask me to come over."

She made a small sound in her throat. "And when I do that, you'll just fly in from L.A. or wherever, right?"

"No, I'll drive from across town."

She tried to turn around. Only he held her fast.

"No, don't. If you look at me while we're sitting on this bed I won't be able to do what I know I have to do. For both of us."

Jena didn't say anything for a long moment, trying to register what he had said.

"That's right. I bought a condo on the other side of town. I'm staying in Albuquerque, Jena."

Relief so full and complete and confusing suffused her body and made her dizzy.

"But…"

"But what? The game? If you'd looked beyond the jock you saw every time you came through that door, the jock you welcomed into your bed every night but banned from your heart, I might have told you that I was seriously considering not returning to the game."

"But I thought…I mean, hockey is your life."

"No, hockey was my hobby. Something I chose over medicine back in college. But it doesn't give me the same thrill anymore. And when I ran into Noah again…''

''The guy I met at the hockey game.''

''Yes.''

Jena sat pole still, trying to absorb all he was saying. ''You mean…you're a doctor?''

A quiet, humorless chuckle sounded behind her. ''Don't sound so surprised.''

She shrugged from his grasp and turned to face him. ''Well, what did you expect? You never said anything, Tommy.''

His face was drawn in serious lines. ''You never asked, Jena. You just always assumed I was a brainless jock who thought with his willy instead of his head.''

She looked down at the bedspread. ''I happen to like Willy,'' she whispered, then gave him a provocative look.

She heard what sounded like a grudging groan. ''I like Willy too but contrary to popular belief I usually don't let him run my life.''

She noticed the tightness in his strong jaw, the darkening of his eyes and felt an answering response inside her.

He swore with unerring conviction. ''Damn it. That's why I didn't want you to look at me when I told you this.''

Jena slowly blinked, then gazed at him through half-lidded eyes. ''Why, Tommy?''

This time he did groan as he slid his fingers into her hair. "This was never meant to be a permanent thing, this visit. I should have left a couple of days after I came." His voice dropped to a stimulating whisper. "But somehow even knowing all that, I couldn't bring myself to leave."

Jena averted her gaze and smiled. "And I knew I should have asked you to leave, but I couldn't bring myself to do that either." She looked at him straight on. "What do you think that means?"

He ever so slowly leaned forward and kissed her. But when she would have deepened the kiss, he pulled back. "Because the sex is so incredible?"

Frustrated by his physical rebuff, she scooted closer to him on the bed, not stopping until a whisper of air separated them. "Oh, yes. There's that," she agreed, brushing her mouth against his again, sliding her hands inside his sweatshirt and pressing her palms flat against his hard male nipples. She started to say something more, but the words fluttered out of reach. So instead she moved one of her hands toward the fly of his jeans. He caught her wrist in his hand.

"And what else, Jena?"

Her breath caught in her throat at the intense expression on his handsome face. "What?"

"What stopped you from asking me to leave and me from leaving?"

She shifted uncomfortably, the move only heightening the growing ache in her belly. "Lack of opportunity?"

His hand still holding her wrist, she tunneled her fingers under the soft denim, her fingertips touching the knob of his satin heat just beyond. He was hot for her, which made her all the hotter for him.

She eased her hand farther into his jeans then fully cupped him.

Air hissed from between his teeth. "You know, from the minute I met you, I thought you were going to be the death of me." He still held her wrist but didn't try to stop her as she methodically unbuttoned his jeans. "My only fear is that you won't admit the real reason why neither of us reacted the way we normally would until it was too late."

Jena vaguely registered what he said as she reached in for his hard arousal. "I think it's time we free Willy, don't you?"

13

JENA CALLED FOR ONE OF the interns to bring her a file, then strategically placed it on the conference table that was already filled with other files.

The War Room. The smaller of the two conference rooms at the firm had been temporarily transformed into the central holding and meeting place having anything to do with the Glendale case. Jena collapsed into one of the ten chairs circling the table and rubbed the skin between her eyes, trying to ease the tension there. Three days into the trial and she felt like they'd been going at it for three weeks.

She'd long ago learned that cases inexplicably either went your way or they didn't. On some rare occasions they traveled down the mediocre middle road without leaving much impression either way.

This case was definitely not going her way.

Every witness the assistant D.A. called had been articulate, clear and eminently believable, and when Jena had questioned them, she'd been the one to come off looking like she had something to hide, willing to go to any lengths to free her client, which included baiting and leading the witnesses. This afternoon

Judge Madison had even threatened to find her in contempt if she kept up what the judge referred to as her "antics" in the courtroom.

And throughout it all Patsy sat neatly coiffed and dressed, her hands folded in her lap, her posture reflecting only the finest finishing school.

Marie came into the War Room, scanned the files already on the table, then dumped another one on top of it. She sighed, then dropped into a chair across the table from Jena. They sat there for what seemed like a long time, neither of them saying anything, both of them considering the organized mess on the table.

Marie finally sighed and looked at her watch. "It's almost nine-thirty already. Should I order up some dinner?"

Jena closed her eyes and stretched her neck, thinking that Tommy would have something waiting at home for her…

She blinked her eyes open. Three days had passed since he'd left and she still sometimes forgot he wasn't there anymore.

"Sure," she said, sitting up. "Pizza is the safest bet at this hour." She glanced at her own watch.

"Already have them on autodial." Marie spoke the word "pie" into her cell phone then placed the order.

"Pie?" Jena asked. "Why not pizza?"

Marie clipped the phone back to the waist of her skirt. "Because I already had my cousin programmed in as 'pizzaface.'"

Jena managed a halfhearted laugh, feeling exhausted all the way down to her bones.

Although if she gave it half a thought, she'd probably discover that, yes, while she had been working hard, there was something more to blame for her lethargy than just the trial.

"You know something is wrong with that dog. Normally any other mutt would be chewing up everything in the place," Marie said quietly.

Jena glanced at where Caramel was stretched out on the floor, her head on her front paws, her eyes moving as she looked at Marie, then Jena, then back again. She gave a gusty sigh then closed her eyes altogether.

Jena sighed along with her. Caramel had been like that ever since Tommy had left. And, oh boy, could she ever relate.

"I know I shouldn't have brought her in here. But the girl who usually looks after her has gone skiing with her family for the holidays and I didn't have any other choice."

"Oh?"

Jena gave her friend a pointed look. "Don't 'oh?' me."

Marie gestured dismissively with her hand. "That was a 'you don't say' kind of oh. Only I didn't have the energy to say it."

Jena rubbed her closed eyelids, listening as two of the three interns who had stayed late talked quietly in the lobby while they made reams of copies. Somewhere Mona rattled around as well, as did Barry. Jena vaguely wondered if they were hanging out in the bathroom together again. "Yes, Tommy's gone."

Marie didn't immediately say anything, so Jena opened her eyes to look at her.

"Gone as in gone away to play a football game?"

"It's hockey and you know it."

Marie made a face. "Gone as in forever, or gone as in the visit's over?"

"The latter. And well put."

Marie seemed to mentally chew on the info. "So he went back to L.A. then."

"No. He's still here."

Marie brows rose. "Here as in…"

"Albuquerque."

Marie slumped in her chair. "Jena, I really don't have the strength for this. Stop acting like a reluctant witness and give it up."

Jena pretended an interest in her fingernails and her need for a good manicure. "There's nothing to give up. He left the apartment, moved into his own place, and I haven't heard from him since." She cleared her throat. "Oh, and he's also a doctor."

Marie snapped forward. "What?"

"You heard me. It, um, seems he earned a medical degree in college and is joining a practice here in town. He's specializing in sports medicine."

"Tommy 'Wild Man' Brodie is going to be a doctor?"

Jena grimaced. "Yes, so it would seem."

They both fell silent for long moments, listening to the noise and lack of it coming from the offices and Caramel's muted sighing sounds.

Marie laughed softly.

"What?"

Her friend lazily shrugged her slender shoulders. "I don't know. Call me crazy, but I think you're the only one who can get a guy to completely move his life to where you are and you think it's a sign that things are over."

Jena rolled her eyes to stare at the ceiling. "Very funny. And that's not even close to what happened."

"So why haven't you called him?"

Jena pushed up from the chair, searching for that all-important tenth wind so that she could finish preparing for her first defense witness tomorrow. Oh, yes, Tommy had left his number with her. In fact, he'd left three numbers with her. The one to his cell, the one to his condo, and the one to the medical offices where he would unofficially be working until the end of the hockey season and his retirement from the game. He'd also given her his address. Last night at one in the morning she'd driven way out of her way to go by the place. The light had been on in his apartment, but she hadn't gone up. In fact, she had accelerated the car for fear that he might spot her and think she was stalking him.

God, what a mess all this had turned out to be.

She cleared her throat and glared at Marie. "In case you haven't noticed, we've been a little busy lately."

"Oh, I've noticed." Marie also got up from her chair and started going through the files on her side of the table looking for something. "But a trial hasn't stopped you from having a personal life before."

A personal life. Boy, now that was a vague topic heading, wasn't it? And one Tommy Brodie didn't come near fitting under. She'd always viewed her personal life as a never-ending series of hit-and-run encounters with nary a commitment in sight on either side of the equation.

Tommy had definitely qualified as an "encounter" the first time they met the night of Dulcy's bachelorette party. And Jena had tried to pretend he still fit the criteria the night he showed up on the other side of her door wearing that naughty grin of his. But she was slowly coming to realize that somewhere between the first encounter and the second, something had changed in her. After that one night, her "personal life," as Marie had put it, had changed. It wasn't just that she had stopped dating, she'd even stopped shopping. It was as if some secret internal list had been satisfied the instant she and Tommy met. And once complete, the list disappeared, leaving her alone to figure out the rest of it on her own.

She made a face. Philosophy was so not her area. Neither was self-analyzing. Following the loss of her parents she'd gone to live with her aunt, who was financially in the same class her parents had been in but made a point of staying out of it. She'd been made to go to a child psychologist twice a week in the beginning, once a week for a year after that. Time after time the psychologist would tell her to write her thoughts in a journal. Time after time she came in with the journal pages filled with squiggly lines and her and her friends names scribbled across the white space. She was told she needed to purge whatever she was feeling so she could move on. She'd told the psychologist that she didn't have anything to purge. What had happened was an unfortunate accident, as everyone kept saying to her. No, she didn't feel she was to blame. No, she didn't think there was anything she could have done to stop the event from happening. And no, she didn't delude herself into thinking her parents were coming back. They were gone. It was as simple as that.

And if the legal system and society would have been then what it was today, she might not have lost her mother along with her father. She might not have grown up with an emotionally detached aunt because her mother had thought being an orphan would be better than having a mother serving life in prison— or worse, being executed by lethal injection.

If she had any lingering issues that stemmed from

the loss of her parents, she didn't recognize them. And didn't want to start now.

And she certainly didn't want to think about some subconscious wish list that had been met by Tommy Brodie.

"I'm not going to call him."

She didn't realize that she'd said the words aloud until Marie blinked at her. "What did you say?"

Jena stared at her point blank. "I said I'm not going to call him." She stacked a file on top of another one with a loud smack. "I don't want a man in my life right now, not full-time."

"Jena, you've never had a man in your life full-time."

"Exactly." She shoved the files until they sat in the middle, perfectly parallel, with the files on either side of them. "What do I know about being in a relationship? I've never had to call anyone to let them know I'll be late. Or explain why I'm breaking a date. Or wanted to buy them gifts." She glanced at her friend. "Aside from you and Dulcy, that is."

"I knew what you meant."

She sighed and shifted her weight from one foot to the other. "Do you think that some people just aren't built for marriage?"

Marie's eyes widened.

"I mean, if you don't think you want children, and you like your life the way it is, doesn't it just make sense to avoid that whole route?"

"You don't want children?"

Jena gave a gusty sigh. "I don't know, Marie. I just asked you a question. Don't answer it with another one or my brain will explode and you won't be able to read all these files because of the gray matter splattered all over them."

"Now there's an image."

Jena gave a small smile, then laughed.

"I don't know," Marie finally said, making a note on her pad, then turning the page of the file she was thumbing through. "While, personally, the thought scares me, maybe you're right. Some people might not be meant for marriage."

Jena felt like an incredible weight had been lifted from her shoulders.

"However," Marie said, lifting a finger for emphasis, "I don't happen to believe you're one of them."

Jena glared at her friend, feeling very much like crawling across the table and strangling her.

"Who isn't one of what?" Barry asked, breezing into the room and bringing the mild scent of expensive cologne with him.

"You really don't expect anyone to answer that question, do you?" Jena sighed.

Barry chuckled as he put an arm around her shoulders. "If anyone's capable of answering any question out there, it's you, Jena."

"I wouldn't be too sure about that," she said under

her breath, then smiled at him as if she'd said something entirely different. "Where's Mona?"

A shadow passed over his handsome features. "How should I know?"

Jena bit back the desire to say that if anyone would know, he would, but a glance at Marie as she tore a sheet of paper from her notepad and crumpled it up told her she was likely the only person outside the couple in question who knew what was going on.

And what was likely no longer going on.

Jena leaned closer to Barry. "Trouble in quickie land?"

Barry nearly choked as he stared at her, then at Marie, who hadn't heard what she'd said.

"Someone order pizza?" Mona said, entering the room with two large boxes in her hands.

"Oh, you're a saint," Marie said on a long sigh as she put her notepad aside and helped Mona set out the pizza on the side table; Caramel watched her with mild interest but did little more than sluggishly wag her tail.

Barry blinked. "What's a dog doing in here?"

Marie and Jena looked at each other. "Dog?" Jena asked as Marie used a piece of pepperoni to tempt the hungry canine to the other side of the table and out of sight. "What dog?"

Barry's mouth turned up in that knowing little smile. "Mona, a round of soft drinks for everyone."

Mona appeared not to hear him as she headed for the door. "Get it yourself. I'm going home."

Everyone stood rooted to the spot, silent. Mona had never talked to anyone like that, much less Barry. She was always Mona-on-the-spot, ready to fill any request. Now they all listened to her gather her purse from her desk drawer like she did every night, then the front office door close after her.

"What's gotten into her?" Marie asked.

Jena crossed her arms and eyed Barry. What, indeed?

TOMMY UNLOCKED THE DOOR to his condo and let himself in. A flick of a switch and the place came to life. Amazing what a bit of money in the right hands could accomplish in a short amount of time. A local decorator had arranged for a furniture store to fill his apartment with loaners until the pieces he'd ordered arrived in a month. Being in the southwest, he'd satisfied his desire to go whole hog with the American Indian motif. Warm, hand-woven rugs covered the pale wood floors, tapestries hung on the walls and pueblo pottery stood on the fireplace hearth. In the master bedroom, he'd gone the mission route without the footboard because he would have had to sleep curled in a fetal position in order to fit. The guest room-slash-office held a desk and a futon.

He rubbed his chin, thinking the decorator had done well.

The only problem was, even brimming with furniture, plants, throws and accent pieces, the place felt empty.

He tossed a file to the foyer table and shrugged out of his jacket on the way to the bedroom. It was more than that he was unfamiliar with the place. It was that it wasn't Jena's. He'd never seen himself being comfortable with the art deco look, the stark lines, the dark veneers of her apartment, but somehow just knowing the place was hers, and having her in it, made it feel like home.

Home.

He grimaced and checked his answering machine. One message was from his older sister asking what he was doing in Albuquerque. The other message was from a telemarketer. He sighed and saved the one from his sister to remind himself to call her tomorrow; the other he erased. If he was disappointed that Jena hadn't called, he wasn't going to admit it to himself. The truth was he'd known she wouldn't call within the first few days. She was too proud for that, too convinced that she had to prove something to him and to herself. Namely, that she didn't need anyone but herself. A single woman in charge of her own destiny.

Labels. He'd always hated them. You were either a jock or an intellectual. Single or married. Independent or codependent. Never both or somewhere in between. He stepped into the kitchen, thinking about how Jena had made, and was making, the mistake of labeling. And thinking how much her attitude had affected him when he'd always been quietly amused by it before.

He made himself a turkey breast sandwich on whole wheat and looked down at the floor, only then realizing he had expected Caramel to be there waiting for a tidbit.

Damn.

He glanced at his watch as he took his sandwich into the living room and sat down in front of the coffee table. It was still before midnight. How would Jena feel if he called her now? Or, even better, stopped by for a surprise visit…?

No. He'd promised both himself and her that he wouldn't do that.

Maybe just this once…

There was rap at the apartment door. Tommy halted midchew, his pulse instantly kicking up. Could he and Jena be on the same wavelength? Could that be her finally realizing they had something more than a sometimes thing? Or was she just looking for a little bit of that sometimes thing right now?

He wiped his mouth and quickly moved to the door to find out.

14

TOMMY DIDN'T FIND Jena standing on the other side of the door. Instead he stared at Kostas Volanis looking like he'd traveled halfway across the country and back and hadn't fared very well.

"God, man, aren't you going to invite a guy in after he just spent the past ten hours on planes and in airports?"

Tommy frowned and motioned his soon to be ex-sports agent inside. "By all means, come in."

"Now there's a welcome." Kostas stepped inside, dropping his overnight bag on the floor and shrugging out of his overcoat. "I swear, that's the last time I decide to head to the airport and wing it so close to the holidays. Nice place."

Tommy crossed his arms over his chest and watched Kostas look over the apartment. At thirty-two, nearly as tall as Tommy, with jet-black hair, black eyes and Mediterranean features, there was no doubting Kostas's Greek heritage.

There was also no doubting the reason he was here.

"I'm not going to change my mind, K," Tommy said, cutting right to the chase.

Kostas blinked at him then grinned. "Who said that's why I'm here?"

"I say."

"Can't I have stopped by just to see my old buddy, old pal, old friend?"

"No. An old buddy, old pal, old friend doesn't spend ten hours taking a two-hour trip just to stop by."

Kostas chuckled and held up his hands. "Okay, okay. But can a guy get a cup of coffee before we get into all this?"

Tommy narrowed his eyes. "I'm still deciding whether or not I want to kick your butt back out into the hall and call you a cab back to the airport."

Kostas ignored him and stepped into the living room. "You have a spare room in this joint, don't you? No matter. The couch looks big enough for one night."

"Confident, aren't you?"

Kostas raised a brow. "Have you known me to be different?"

Tommy finally gave in and ran his hand through his hair. Kostas hadn't gotten where he was by being a pushover. And he hadn't gotten to be Tommy's friend because he was easy to resist. Yes, Kostas was persistent. But he was also loyal, smart and worth a lot of laughs.

"A little coffee with your sugar, right?"

"Right. Thanks."

"Don't mention it. Depending on what you have to say, you might not get to finish it."

Kostas dropped down onto the southwestern-style sofa then lifted a finger. "Ah, my dear friend, you underestimate me. You don't think I'd come if I didn't have an offer not even you could refuse, do you?"

Tommy winced. No, he didn't. And given the way things were progressing here in Albuquerque—or not progressing—Tommy was afraid he was open to just such an offer....

THERE WAS SOMETHING ABOUT courthouses that gave Jena goose bumps. The good kind. No matter how much time she spent in them, or how badly a case was going, she had but to smell the wood polish, appreciate the shine of the floor and she virtually felt the importance seep into her bones. This was where decisions were made concerning every American's life. Where death sentences were meted out or liberty granted. Where laws were tested and rewritten and enforced.

Where, within one blink of an eye, with one unexpected witness, the tides could change in your favor or turn into a tsunami and come after you.

Judge Madison had called a fifteen-minute morning break between witnesses. Jena spoke to Marie for a moment, then ducked out into the hall, watching as spectators and prospective jurors from the next courtroom walked the hallowed halls. It was at times like these that she wished she were a smoker so she could join the rest of them filing outside for a quick one and a little conversation. People around the ashtrays seemed to be a social, welcoming bunch.

This morning she and the entire defense team had bounced back with a vengeance. She'd presented three unshakable witnesses that spoke of the sharp verbal abuse Patsy Glendale had suffered through from her husband, and even testified about having seen evidence of possible physical abuse. Throughout the testimony, she'd carefully watched the jury, trying to read their expressions, crawl inside their heads. At the very least they had appeared open to the testimony—which was a good thing. She'd been involved in her share of trials in which the jurors had sat stone-faced with their arms crossed over their chests, unwilling to hear a single favorable word in defense.

Jena slipped her cell phone from her purse then placed a quick call to Mona for a phone number, then dialed the number for the firm's private detective who had been out of contact recently.

"Sure thing, Ms. McCade. I'll put you right through," Jo Logan's secretary said.

Jena heaved a sigh of relief and waited as she was put on hold.

The motivation for her call was twofold. To make sure the assistant D.A. didn't have an ace up his sleeve in the shape of Lorena Taylor, law student and

Harrison Glendale's mistress. No matter the laws regarding discovery and producing witnesses, merely showing her to the jury could damage her case immeasurably.

And the other reason she was calling was to establish whether the reason the D.A. hadn't introduced her so far was because she was damaging to the prosecution's case.

She absently chewed her bottom lip. If Lorena Taylor was damaging to the prosecution's case, then that meant she could possibly be a credit to Patsy's.

"Any luck?" Marie asked, coming out of the courtroom. She'd tried to find Lorena Taylor for the past week with no luck. The address listings for her had been dead-ends, and the phone number listed at the University of New Mexico's School of Law had come up disconnected.

"I'm on hold now," Jena said.

Marie nodded. "I'm going to get a Diet Coke. You want something?"

"Hmm? No, I'm fine. Thanks."

Jena absently watched Marie walk down the hall looking much like a lighted matchstick with her thin build, pale skin and curly red, red hair. Jena glanced at her watch, hoping the P.I. would pick up before she was due back in court.

"Jena."

She let out a sigh of relief at the sound of the private investigator's voice on the line. "Jo. Hi. Boy, getting through to you is next to impossible. Don't you have a cell phone?''

''Don't believe in them. You know how easy the conversations you have on them are to monitor? Forget bugs. All you need is a twenty-dollar radio from The Sharper Image and you're privy to the most intimate conversations between two people.''

Jena lifted her brows. ''Oh, thanks for giving me another reason not to sleep well at night.''

''Don't mention it.''

Some of the spectators started filing back into the courtroom. Jena moved a little farther down the hall and smiled as one of the prosecution team walked by her.

''Look, Jo, I won't keep you long. I just have a quick question, then I'll let you get back to what you were doing.''

''Fire away.''

''The information you provided on Lorena Taylor…you didn't include contact information. Any particular reason why?''

''I thought you knew.''

''Knew what?''

''That she's living at the Glendale place.''

Jena nearly dropped the phone. ''What?'' She tried to digest the information and all it suggested. The husband's mistress living under the same roof as the wife? A chilling shudder ran the length of Jena's spine.

"Yes," Jo said. "She's been staying there for the past eight months."

Jena calculated that that was two months before Patsy had shot her husband. "He moved his mistress into the family home? My God, I probably would have killed him myself."

"His mistress?" the P.I. said with an obvious smile in her voice. "Jena, Harrison Glendale wasn't the one having the affair with Lorena Taylor. Patsy was. And apparently still is."

TOMMY WASN'T SURE WHAT had made him go to the courthouse. He supposed he just wanted to see Jena in her home venue. Hell, he just wanted to see Jena, period. The trial had been covered to a great extent in the local news since it had begun and it had been torture to watch her flash a smile into the camera as she left the courthouse, never saying more than, "I have every confidence we'll prove our case," or, "Soon it will be in the jury's capable hands."

He'd never been to a courthouse before but he doubted many looked like the new seven-story modern complex in which he stood. He assumed all the courtrooms were in session because the halls were eerily silent. He stopped a security guard and asked him which courtroom the Glendale trial was in. Within moments he was quietly opening the door at the back of the courtroom and scanning the interior.

He stepped inside and found a seat in the back—the only seat left.

"Please state and spell your name for the court." Marie took a Bible from the stand as she addressed the witness taking a seat behind it.

Where was Jena? He looked at the two tables in front of the judge's bench. There. To the left. Jena had her head bent over notes, an empty chair to her left, and the woman of the hour, Patsy Glendale, was sitting next to that one.

Tommy sat back and crossed his arms. He really didn't have an opinion one way or the other as to the guilt or innocence of Glendale. He hadn't paid that close attention to the news coverage and aside from the few occasions the topic had come up between him and Jena, he'd decided he wasn't that curious. No, his attention then and now had been on the beautifully provocative defense attorney.

He squinted as Jena lifted her head. She looked tired, which wasn't surprising four days into the trial. But he suspected there was something more behind her exhausted expression. Dare he hope it was because she missed him?

The woman next to him, a grandmotherly type in a red jogging suit, leaned against his side. "Guilty as dirt," she whispered to him.

A young woman in the next bench turned to glare at her.

Tommy leaned toward the older woman. "How guilty is dirt?"

"Guilty," she said, nodding her head emphatically.

Tommy tapped his finger against his lips to suppress the grin threatening and turned his attention back to Jena.

Damn, she looked good. Tired, but good. It seemed like months had passed since he'd last touched her, even though it had only been five days. Her raven-black hair shone under the ceiling lights, her pale skin was almost luminescent, and the tailored suit she wore hugged her in all the right places. Oh, what he wouldn't give to press his mouth against the curve of her neck just then. He glanced at the bench. Somehow he didn't think the judge would appreciate it.

Marie finished with the witness, making Tommy realize he hadn't heard a thing either she or the witness had said.

"Permission to approach, Your Honor?" Jena said, getting to her feet.

The judge motioned for both lead counsel to come to stand in front of the bench.

A moment later the judge banged his gavel. "The court will stand in recess until one-fifteen."

Tommy frowned and glanced at his watch. It was only ten forty-five. A little early for lunch, wasn't it? And long.

He watched the defendant being led from the courtroom by armed sheriff's deputies then switched his gaze back to Jena who was saying something to Marie and packing up her stuff.

"Excuse me," the woman next to him said, getting up and practically climbing over his long legs to get toward the aisle. Tommy chuckled and rose himself, only he was prevented from leaving because the woman was blocking his way as she conversed with an elderly man in the row in front of them.

Tommy cleared his throat, but she didn't appear to notice. He cleared his throat again.

"Oh, I'm sorry," she said. "Did you want through?"

She moved out of the way and Tommy stepped into the aisle…and straight into Jena's path.

"Tommy," she said, her voice soft and breathless.

Her reaction made the risk of coming here worth it. Her skin immediately flushed, her violet eyes lit up and her mouth turned up in a spontaneous smile.

He cleared his throat again, this time for altogether different reasons. "Um, I thought I'd stop by and see you in your home court."

"Literally," she said.

People were trying to move by both of them. Tommy motioned toward the door. "Can I treat you to lunch?"

All the light disappeared from her face as she looked around, then back into his face. "I can't."

Tommy felt decidedly uncomfortable. Okay, so he hadn't meant to see her when he came down here.

But there was no way she could know that. He hadn't experienced rejection often, but he determined that he didn't like it. Not at all.

"I understand."

"No, no. It's not like that."

Tommy held her gaze. "You know where I'm at, Jena. But I can't promise you how long I'll be there."

Her brows lifted in surprise.

"Jena? Oh." Marie peered around her friend to see what the hold up was. She smiled wide when she saw it was Tommy.

Tommy said a quick hello then turned and left the courtroom and Jena behind.

"PATSY GLENDALE IS NOT your mother, Jena."

Jena stared wide-eyed at Marie, feeling suddenly like she'd been hit in the solar plexus. "What?" she whispered.

Their surroundings in the homey family-owned restaurant vanished, seeming to leave her and Marie in some sort of vacuum-packed alternate reality. She just finished telling her friend and cocounsel what she'd learned from the P.I. After a long pause, Marie had made her shocking comment, nearly knocking from Jena's mind even the memory of Tommy's face as he'd turned and left her standing in the courtroom. Nearly.

Marie rested her forearms on the table and leaned forward. "You heard me." She sighed. "Look, Jena, from the get-go I wondered about your motivations for taking this case. Oh sure, you'd have me and Dulcy and Barry believe that you were doing it for the publicity it would bring the firm. High-profile case. Media interest.'' She bit briefly on her bottom lip as if considering whether or not she should continue.

Jena gestured with her hand. "Oh, by all means, continue. There's no getting that cat back into the bag." She straightened her shoulders, ready to defend herself.

Marie grimaced. "Oh, no. Now you're getting all prickly."

"Prickly is my normal mode of operation."

"Not with me, it isn't." She sighed. "Okay, if you're going to be pissed at me, I might as well give you reason to be—Patsy Glendale is guilty as dirt."

"Dirt?"

Marie shrugged. "One of the court groupies uses the saying all the time. Anyway, she's guilty. No ifs ands or buts about it. I've felt that way since the beginning. And the only reason you prefer to ignore that little fact is that you see Patsy as your mother somehow. Get Patsy off and in some misguided way you think you'll be saving your mother."

Jena's back came against the booth. "That's just so much crap."

Marie sat up. "Is it?"

Jena stared at her friend for a long moment, trying

to decide whether to say something offensive and storm out of the restaurant...or vent on her all the conflicting emotions she'd been feeling lately. About everything. Not just the case, but her parents' deaths, Tommy, her inability to break through the wall that wouldn't let her commit to anyone beyond her friends.

Jena let out the breath she was holding in a long, drawn-out gust, then sagged forward. "Oh, God, Marie. You know, I'm afraid you're right."

Marie couldn't have looked more shocked had Jena just dumped her salad into her lap.

Jena rested her head against her hand, suddenly so thoroughly exhausted it was a chore not to curl up in the booth and drop off to sleep. "I've been carrying around all this...I don't know, darkness for so long." She rolled her eyes when they started to water. "God, I'm so pathetic."

"No, you're not." Marie took her hand.

Jena reached for the napkin holder with her free hand and began taking napkins out. "I keep thinking that, you know, if I don't let myself get too close to anyone that I'll never hurt again the way I did when my parents died." She'd nearly emptied out the napkin holder and stared unseeingly at the mountain of white paper she had made. "God, I couldn't have been more wrong. When I saw Tommy in the courtroom today... Oh, Marie, he looked so good and I wanted him so much. Despite everything happening with the trial and the case, in that one minute I wanted to chuck everything and run off with him.''

Marie smiled. ''Then why didn't you?''

''Because I can't.''

The smile slowly left Marie's face. ''Sure, you can. All you have to—''

''You're not hearing me,'' Jena said resolutely. ''I can't. There's something inside me that won't let me. Something that scares me to death.''

They sat there like that for long minutes, neither of them saying anything, neither of them eating the meals the waitress had put in front of them, merely contemplating what the other had said.

Battling against the tightness in her chest, Jena finally removed her hand from Marie's and sat back. She took a deep, shaky breath. ''I can't believe I just said all that.''

''Neither can I.''

Jena met Marie's gaze and they both smiled softly.

''You know, if you need anything, any time of the day or night, I'm there for you, you know that, don't you? And so is Dulcy.''

''I know. You guys…you've been the only constants in my life. And I'm grateful for that.''

''But you can't take my advice?''

Jena shook her head and tried to put in order the mess she'd made with the napkins, as if by doing so she could make sense out of the emotional mess roiling inside her. ''No.''

"Fine." Marie shrugged and pulled her plate back in front of her. "Suffer then."

Jena stared at her. That was such an un-Marielike thing to say.

"I'm sorry. I'm not going to feel for you on this one, Jena. Because given everything I've seen and heard, Tommy sounds like he's exactly what you need in your life right now. And you're determined to screw it up." She shrugged again as she took a bite of her salad. "You're all alone on this one, babe."

As soon as the shock of what her friend had said passed, a strange kind of…freedom settled over Jena's limbs.

For so long her friends had been careful around her. Watchful of what they said, what they did, even though years had passed since the loss of her parents. There was a time when Jena had tried to shock a more honest reaction from them, prod them into a fight, into normal responses. Make them yell at her and tell her she was acting like an idiot.

Neither of them ever had.

She smiled. Until now.

"So what are you going to do about the info you received on Glendale?" Marie broke into her thoughts.

Jena blinked her back into focus. "I don't know." She looked at her watch. "If I get back to the court-

house, I can talk to her before the court is called back
to order.''

''And then?''

''And then...'' She drifted off. ''We can win this,
you know.''

''I know. The question is, do we want to?''

Jena gathered her things together without having
eaten anything. ''To win or not to win. That's the
question.'' She got up. ''But that's not the only option.''

15
___

TOMMY ACCEPTED THE BEER the bartender handed
him, then knocked back a good portion of it as he
waited for Noah to join him. He'd just returned from
driving Kostas to the airport to catch the next flight
back to L.A. He'd done so without giving his friend
and agent an answer to the offer he'd put on the table.

And what an offer it was.

Kostas hadn't been kidding when he'd said he had
something not even Tommy could turn down. Essentially he'd contacted the owner of the L.A. Aces and
told him of Tommy's intentions to retire at year's end.
The Aces had offered to triple his salary, with a
healthy bonus if they made it to the finals next season.
The pay hike would make him the highest paid player
in the NHL by far—and the most sought after for
commercial endorsements.

The catch, and there always was one, was that he'd
have to sign for three years.

He absently rubbed his recovering knee, thinking
of all the players who would give their right eye for
such a sweet deal. He continued to rub his knee. But
three more years on the ice. Traveling from city to

city. Staying in countless cookie-cutter hotel rooms. Risking more serious injury.

Funny, before he would think only of the thrill of being on the ice. Now he saw only the risks, the tedium.

But in this latest offer he also saw an opportunity for him to forget about one certain, frustrating Ms. Jena McCade.

He glanced around the upscale sports bar. The large-screen televisions covering the walls flashed every event imaginable to man. The after-work crowd began to fill the thick oak tables. Behind the bar, the bartender reached up and changed his set to the local news.

"Hey, turn it up, man," a guy a few stools down from Tommy called.

The bartender did as requested as the news cut to a commercial for a used-car dealership.

"What's up?" Noah asked as he joined Tommy. He took the stool next to him and shrugged out of his coat.

"Thanks for coming," Tommy said.

Noah asked the bartender to bring him what Tommy was having. "Don't mention it. It sounded important."

Tommy twirled his bottle around on the surface of the raw, unpolished bar. "I thought you and I should have a talk."

"Uh-oh. Sounds ominous." Noah accepted a beer from the bartender. "You're not having second thoughts, are you?"

Tommy didn't say anything, merely sat staring at his bottle.

Noah sighed. "You know, you're not obligated to me for anything, Tom. We haven't had the papers drawn up yet. And while I'm sure we'll continue with the plans you were putting together for a more comprehensive rehabilitation center, if you're thinking about opting out..."

Noah drifted off. Tommy squinted at him. "If I'm thinking of opting out?"

His longtime friend frowned. "Well, then, that's your prerogative." He leaned back and patted his suit jacket pocket, the movements of an ex-smoker, even though he'd quit the habit five years ago. "Look, Tommy, I won't pretend to understand what's going through your head right now. Until last fall and the exhibition game, I didn't even know you knew where Albuquerque was. Then up and out of the blue you show up on my doorstep to continue your physical therapy and say you're going to be in town for a while." He grinned. "Of course I jumped at the opportunity to try to pull you into the practice. You graduated near the top of the class. Well above me." He shook his head. "And then you didn't even become a doctor."

Tommy grinned.

"Are you thinking about returning to the game?"

He sighed. "Yeah, I am. But not for the reasons you might think."

"The offer that good, huh?"

Tommy paused. "For many reasons, yes. And I'm not talking about the money."

Noah nodded silently.

Tommy's attention drifted to the flickering television set as the news came back on. He was trying to word his apology to Noah and his gratitude for all he had done when a picture of Jena flicked on in the upper right-hand corner of the screen, behind the newscaster.

"Tommy, I—"

"Shh."

Noah lifted his brows but went quiet as the newscaster continued speaking.

"…an interesting development to report tonight in the Glendale case. After the midday recess, attorney Jena McCade returned to the courtroom and requested removal as Patsy Glendale's attorney of record. As you'll recall, Ms. Glendale is on trial for the murder of her late husband…"

Tommy stared at the screen without hearing the rest of the newscaster's comments. He merely watched a clip of Jena and Marie exiting the courthouse together, smiling into the camera and offering no comment as the media descended on them like a bunch of vultures.

"Wait a minute," Noah said, having followed Tommy's attention on the news. "Isn't that the woman I met at the hockey game?"

Tommy didn't answer. All he could do was wonder why Jena pulled out of the case. And what it would mean to her career.

"Yes," he said, finally answering Noah's question. He peeled off a couple of large bills and tossed them onto the bar. "I've got to go."

TWO HOURS LATER, Tommy was ready to climb the walls—if there'd been any walls around to climb. He put his rental car into park outside his new apartment, then shut off the engine. Dusk had long since fallen, and outside a light fog was starting to crowd around the warmer ground, giving the night a surreal feel. He'd gone by Jena's apartment, her law firm, and had even driven around for a while trying to figure out where she might have gone to. All without one shred of luck. Not even anyone at her firm had been able to tell him where she'd gone.

Damn.

Damn, damn, damn.

When he'd heard the news on TV, he'd been immediately concerned about her welfare. She'd worked so hard on that case, had put so much into it. Her walking away from it the way she had, at such risk to her career, worried him more than anything had in a long time. Weren't attorneys disbarred for such behavior?

He shuddered at the thought, finding it impossible to envision Jena without her license to practice.

Since Marie had seen her last, he'd asked her how Jena had been when she'd left the office. Marie had smiled and told him Jena was better than she had been in a long, long time.

He didn't quite know what to make out of that one. Jena ate, lived and breathed her career as an attorney. And she'd been determined that this make-or-break case would make her and her friends.

Cursing under his breath, he climbed from his car. He'd try going by her place again later. Maybe even park out on her doorstep. She had to come back sooner or later. Didn't she?

Of course, had anyone thought that about him nearly three weeks ago, they would have been sorely disappointed because he hadn't been back to his place in L.A. since.

But it took a certain someone to do that for someone else. And the only one who matched that criterion for him was Jena.

He climbed the steps to his apartment and got out his keys to let himself in. A sound from inside his apartment made him pause. It almost sounded like a...

He quickly unlocked the door and shoved it open.

Bark. The sound had been a bark.

Tommy crouched down so that he could catch the boxer pup advancing on him at full speed.

"What are you doing here, C?" he murmured, rubbing the dog's small, wiggling body.

A strange weightless sensation began in Tommy's stomach, then twisted until it consumed his entire body.

If Caramel was here...

He stepped into the apartment and closed the door to keep Caramel from getting out. The lights were on. As was the television—a sitcom, if the sound of canned laughter was any indication. He slowly advanced toward the living room. And what he saw there caused a relief so intense, so overwhelming, to slam over him he nearly dropped to his knees.

There, sitting with her legs crossed on his couch, the remote in one hand, tortilla chips in the other, dressed in old sweats, with her hair caught back in a messy ponytail, sat Jena. Dear, sassy, sexy Jena.

Whether she was pretending not to notice he'd returned home, or whether she was truly wrapped up in her own thoughts, he couldn't tell. All he could do was be thankful she was okay.

And be very thankful that she was in his apartment.

Speaking of which...

"Amazing what effect a good story can have on a building manager," Jena said softly, her eyes still on the set across from her.

Tommy cracked a grin. So she did know he'd come in.

"What did you tell him?"

"Her," she corrected.

"Ah."

She finally looked at him. Her violet eyes were so full of emotion he nearly fell over. But no matter how much he wanted to cross to that sofa and cover her body with his, he had to know more.

"What are you doing here, Jena?"

She didn't blink as she cocked a brow. "Do you have to ask?"

Tommy narrowed his gaze, wondering if she'd been drinking. He scanned the contents of the coffee table. Supermarket tabloids, bags of junk food, cookies, a pint of ice cream and a can of Diet Coke.

No alcohol.

"I should think it would be obvious," she said.

"Jena, nothing about you is obvious."

She twisted her lips. "I think there are a lot of people out there who would disagree with you there."

He scanned her face, finding the tiredness he'd seen there earlier in the day at the courtroom gone and healthy color in its wake. "Maybe. But no one who knows you the way I do."

She briefly averted her gaze. "True."

Damn, but she looked good enough to eat. Her hair was usually neatly combed and down, but he decided he liked it back in a messy ponytail with soft tendrils teasing the back of her neck and cheeks.

She put the remote down, then wiped her hands on her sweats. "You know it's funny, but I seem to be at the same crossroads you were about three weeks ago."

"Crossroads?"

"Uh-huh." She patted the couch beside her. "Why don't you sit down?"

He steeled himself against the desire to do just that. He knew if he did, talk would turn to action and, before you knew it, they would fall into the same routine that saw them to where they were right now. Which was pretty much nowhere until Jena admitted some basic, important truths.

He said, "I'm fine right where I am for the moment, thank you."

Her smile was decidedly carnivorous…and thoroughly provocative. Despite what his head needed to know, his body was responding in a way he couldn't hope to deny. He settled on putting it on hold for now.

"Okay," she said slowly, tucking her legs underneath her. "You see, I might need a place to stay for a while." Caramel barked. "Pardon me. Caramel and I might need a place to stay."

"What's the matter with your place?"

She tucked a stray strand of hair behind her ear and smiled.

"You mean aside from the fact that I might

not be able to make the rent soon?'' She shook her head. ''Nothing.''

''What do you mean you might not be able to make the rent?''

She shrugged. ''Just that.'' She slowly traced circles on the back cushion with the tip of her finger. ''Come on, Tommy, I know you know the news. Marie called me on my cell.''

''Hmm. That means you had it on. Why didn't you accept my calls? I must have called a dozen times in the past hour alone.''

She tilted her head in that teasing way that made him wild. ''Well, that would have ruined the surprise, don't you think?''

Oh, yeah, that it definitely would have.

He held up his hands, trying to ward off his growing need to be near her, over her, inside her. ''Look, Jena, I don't know what you have in mind—''

''Tommy, I'm in very grave danger of being disbarred.''

He was shocked into silence as much from her words as from the expression on her face. Rather than the somber expression he might have expected, instead she looked at peace. At peace with her decision and the consequences she now faced.

''What will you do if they do disbar you?''

She shrugged. ''Oh, I don't know. Move in here, I guess.'' She cleared her throat. ''Get a job as a waitress in some coffee shop. Or maybe a bar.''

Jena, a waitress. Tommy rubbed his chin with his index finger and grinned. He could see Jena in a waitress uniform, all right. Preferably a really tight, really short one. But only for him. And only in the privacy of his own bedroom.

"What's so funny?" she asked.

"Oh, nothing." He coughed. "And what makes you think you're welcome to stay here?"

That seemed to shut her up. Apparently it was the last thing she'd expected him to say. But say it he had to. He'd come an inch away from snatching up the Aces's offer. To turn it down for a few more weeks of on-again, off-again sex with Jena, while tempting, would be insane.

"Because you love me," she whispered.

She said the words so quietly he nearly didn't hear her. He nodded. "Yes, Jena, I do. But how I feel has never been an issue."

She straightened her legs out slowly, one by one, until she was sitting properly. "Yes, but I bet you didn't know I loved you."

Damn, it was taking all of his strength not to go to her. "Oh, you're wrong there. I knew you loved me, Jena. You were the one who couldn't admit it—to yourself or me."

She squinted at him as if unable to bring him into focus. "But isn't that what I just did?"

"I don't know," he said, crossing his arms. "Is it?"

For long moments they stayed like that. Her, unmoving on the sofa, appearing not to know where to go from there. Him, rooted to the spot across the room, knowing he should go everywhere but to her.

"Yes, it is," she whispered.

Before he knew what she had in mind, she got up and crossed the room to him, stopping mere millimeters away. He could smell her spicy scent, see the blue glints in her violet eyes. He swallowed hard to keep himself from reaching out to her. To feel her silky hair between his fingers. To cup her breasts in his palms.

"You're not going to make this easy on me, are you?" she murmured, gazing up into his face.

He shook his head, completely incapable of words.

"Well, then, let me make it easier for you," she said, stepping until the tips of her breasts brushed the front of his shirt, her hips grazing his. She leaned forward. But instead of kissing him the way he expected, she flicked her tongue out, dipping it into the corners of his immobile mouth, then running it along the seams.

Good God...

Tommy cleared his throat. "That's sex, Jena. We've never had a problem with sex."

She shook her head. "Oh, no, Tommy. We stopped having sex a long time ago. What we do, what happens when we come together, is called making love."

That was it.

Tommy tunneled his fingers into her hair and hauled her against him, covering her decadent mouth with his, sealing the words she'd said like a bond between them.

She tasted like soda and chips and something sweet. Distantly he realized that the sweetness was her. The sweetness of finally admitting to loving him. The sweetness of giving herself over to him fully, completely and utterly. Trusting him with her heart without condition. Without doubt.

He briefly pulled his head back from her. "Marry me, Jena."

Her eyes widened.

He skimmed his hands down her neck, felt her pulse throbbing at the base, then moved to grasp her shoulders gently. "No, don't think about it. Just tell me what your knee-jerk reaction is. And act on it."

He watched her throat work around a swallow. "My first thought is that you're insane…"

Tommy began to remove his hands.

She caught them and held them fast. "And my second is yes."

Tommy's heart beat once, twice. Then he was sweeping her up into his arms and striding purposefully toward his bedroom.

She sighed against him. "Well, if I had known it would be that easy to get you into the sack…"

Tommy launched her toward the mission-style bed, then followed after, covering her writhing body with

his, ardently kissing her, touching her, feeling her.
And in that instant he knew that he would have done
anything to hear her say the words she had in the
other room. He would have stayed in Albuquerque
and worked in waste management until that one day
when she finally agreed to become his wife.

"Oh," Jena moaned as he cupped her bare breasts
under her sweatshirt, "how I've missed you."

"Not half as much as I've missed you." He held
her gaze for a long moment, saying nothing, merely
taking her in. "Remember when you asked me about
family? Whether or not I wanted kids?"

"Uh-huh," she said quietly.

He grinned as he tugged her pants down over her
hips and off. "I've suddenly decided I want a houseful of them."

"Houseful?" she whispered. "How big a house are
we talking about?"

He reached for her hand and pressed her fingers
against his rock-hard erection. "Big. Very big."

As he touched her slick heat, she made a soft
sound.

"So, um, what do you suppose they'll call me?
You know," she gasped as he thrust a finger into her
dripping wetness, "after, um, we get married? Mrs.
Wild Man Brodie?"

Tommy stared down at her longingly. "Oh, no,
Jena. You deserve your own title. And Wild Woman
would definitely be it."

As he positioned himself to enter her, he realized that was exactly what he'd gotten—a wild woman capable of taming his wild man.

And, oh, what a woman she was. The yin to his yang. The sour to his sweet.

The fire to his ice.

Epilogue

JENA COULDN'T REMEMBER A time when she'd enjoyed Christmas more. She'd only been out to Dulcy and Quinn's ranch once, and the most she could recall was how damn long it had taken to get there. But the three-hour drive had seemed like nothing while sitting next to her husband.

Her husband.

Wow.

She glanced down at her Christmas gift—a five-carat ruby-and-diamond ring to go with the platinum wedding rings etched with ivy they'd chosen together. She tried to summon up a little guilt that her gift to him had been the black silk robe and pants she couldn't resist buying for him, but she couldn't. Recently she seemed incapable of summoning up anything other than pure bliss.

"I can't believe we all flew to Vegas to watch you two get married," Marie said, fingering her wineglass where she, Jena and Dulcy sat at the rough-hewn pine table in the kitchen of Dulcy and Quinn's ranch house. Through the back window they watched Quinn and Tommy where they stood next to a large black stallion, feeding him an apple in slices.

Jena twisted the ring around her finger, finding it impossible not to smile. It seemed she'd been smiling for a week straight, ever since she'd pulled out of the Glendale trial and finally given herself over to the love she felt for Tommy.

"I can't believe it either," she said with a sigh.

Dulcy topped off both their glasses with wine, then poured more milk into her own wineglass. "That I *can* believe. What I can't believe is that you got little more than a slap on the wrist for dropping Glendale cold like that in front of a seated jury."

Jena shuddered, not much up for thinking about that one. She had no idea what she would have done had she been disbarred. The three of them had just thrown in with Barry Lomax. For her to have to bow out so soon...

She lifted her wineglass. "Here's to the law firm of Lomax, Ferris, McCade and Bertelli being the best in Albuquerque in five years."

Dulcy lifted her glass of milk. "I'll settle for being in the black."

Marie grinned. "I'll take damn good."

The three of them clinked their glasses together, then reflected on what each of them had said.

Marie's chair legs screeched against the tile. "I'll tell you what I can't believe. That Patsy Glendale copped a plea with the D.A. the next day." She shook her head. "Twenty years. Such a small price to pay for murdering your husband in cold blood."

The three friends went silent as they considered

everything that had happened over the past couple of months.

"I invited Barry out," Dulcy said, looking at her watch.

Jena raised her brows. "Did he say he would come?"

She shrugged. "He said he might. I don't know— I kept getting the impression that he had something else on tap, something he didn't want to share."

Jena gave a small smile.

"Uh-oh," Marie said.

"What?"

Dulcy shook her finger at her. "Oh, no, don't even try it, Jena. We both know you too well for that. Spill. What's going on with Barry that we don't know about?"

She blinked several times, feigning innocence. "Whatever do you mean?"

Her two friends stared at her.

"All right, all right." She looked at both of them in turn. "Only I can't tell you what's happening with Barry unless we also discuss what's, um, happening with Mona."

"Mona?" Marie practically squealed. "As in Mona Lyndell, our secretary Mona?"

Jena nodded and the three of them squealed together.

"I knew it," Dulcy said. "I just knew that Mona had a secret crush on him."

"Crush?" Jena said. "I caught the two of them going like gangbusters in the unisex."

"In the bathroom?" Marie said, her eyes bulging. She rubbed her forehead. "God, I don't think I'm going to be able to go into that room again. First Dulcy and Quinn, and now Barry and Mona. God, the place is turning into a regular flophouse."

Dulcy and Jena looked at each other.

"Sounds like someone's getting a little lonely," Jena said quietly.

Marie made a face. "Yeah, this from the woman who slept with a jock and married a doctor."

"Just like the princess who kissed the frog," Dulcy murmured.

Jena smiled. "Yes, but you have to admit I'm no princess and Tommy…" All three of them looked out the window at the wickedly handsome man in question standing with Dulcy's decadently handsome Quinn. "Um, well, Tommy is definitely no frog."

After a long moment, Marie sighed. "Why can't I find a frog of my own?"

Dulcy lifted her glass of milk and held it up. "May your wish be granted," she said.

Jena lifted her wine and Marie quickly followed suit.

All three of them smiled at each other and toasted, "To frogs."

Next month don't miss –

PASSION IN PARADISE

*As the temperature rises and pulses race
faster, three couples surrender to the
heated seduction of an island
in paradise...*

On sale 5th March 2004

0204/05

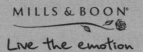

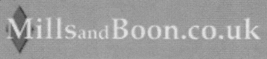

FREE!
2 Books
and a surprise gift!

We would like to take this opportunity to thank you for reading this Mills & Boon® book by offering you the chance to take TWO more specially selected titles, one from the Blaze Romance™ series and one from the Sensual Romance™ series absolutely FREE! We're also making this offer to introduce you to the benefits of the Reader Service™ —

- ★ FREE home delivery
- ★ FREE gifts and competitions
- ★ FREE monthly Newsletter
- ★ Books available before they're in the shops
- ★ Exclusive Reader Service discount

Accepting these FREE books and gift places you under no obligation to buy; you may cancel at any time, even after receiving your free shipment. Simply complete your details below and return the entire page to the address below. **You don't even need a stamp!**

YES! Please send me 2 free Romance books and a surprise gift. I understand that unless you hear from me, I will receive 4 superb new titles every month for just £11.18 (2 Blaze and 2 Sensual), postage and packing free. I am under no obligation to purchase any books and may cancel my subscription at any time. The free books and gift will be mine to keep in any case.

K4ZEE

Ms/Mrs/Miss/Mr ....Initials ....
BLOCK CAPITALS PLEASE

Surname ....

Address ....

....

....Postcode ....

Send this whole page to:
UK: The Reader Service, FREEPOST CN81, Croydon, CR9 3WZ
EIRE: The Reader Service, PO Box 4546, Kilcock, County Kildare (stamp required)